"KEEP YOUR HEAD DOWN!"

Longarm snapped, "Stay put and keep your head down!" as he turned toward the rapid-fire rattle of gunfire with his own gun already drawn.

He stepped out on the platform just as a spidery figure in fusty black dropped off the rear steps of that same Pullman car with a big Schofield .45 in each hand. As the two-gun man shoved a passenger gal on her ass to tear Longarm's way along the platform the experienced lawman had the time to reflect on why so many train robbers favored quick-loading Schofields. So when he yelled, "Stop in the name of the law!" and the wild-eyed stranger threw down on him with his own guns, Longarm simply fired first. Both those Army Issue .45s went off in his general direction as his more tightly aimed .44 slug punched the man in black in the breastbone and off his feet . . .

TABOR EVANS

LONGARM

AND THE WICKED SCHOOLMARM

JOVE BOOKS, NEW YORK

LONGARM AND THE WICKED SCHOOLMARM

A Jove Book / published by arrangement with
the author

PRINTING HISTORY
Jove edition / July 1998

The Penguin Putnam Inc. World Wide Web site address is
http://www.penguinputnam.com

ISBN: 0-515-12302-1

A JOVE BOOK®
Jove Books are published by The Berkley Publishing Group,
a member of Penguin Putnam Inc.,
200 Madison Avenue, New York, New York 10016.
JOVE and the "J" design are trademarks belonging to
Jove Publications, Inc.

PRINTED IN THE UNITED STATES OF AMERICA

10 9 8 7 6 5 4 3 2 1

LONGARM

AND THE WICKED SCHOOLMARM

Chapter 1

Sergeant Nolan of the Denver Police Department knew what *he* was doing there in Cherry Hill Cemetery. He was siding U.S. Deputy Marshal Custis Long as the sun went down behind the Front Range to their west and the moon rose full and pumpkin-colored above the rolling prairie to their east. He just didn't know what *they* were doing there in a deeply shaded cottonwood grove, behind a marble mausoleum, as the last sounds of funeral carriages faded away in the gathering dusk.

Staring out across the staggered ranks of tombstones great and small to where a marble angel held a silent trumpet up to the darkening sky, Nolan unconsciously crossed himself and muttered, "Jesus, Mary, and Joseph and ain't this a cheerful place to be spending such a fine broth of an evening with such a talkative *seanachie*! You told me you'd tell me what this was all about after the last of thim mourners went home and left us alone with a clear view of the dear man's grave! So there lies the late mining magnate Ferris Muldoon under six feet of 'dobe with his tombstone an easy pistol shot from here, and I somehow don't expect to see him rising from his grave at all, at all! Is that what we're here to guard against, Longarm?"

The taller man, better known as Longarm by friend and

1

foe alike, was having his own problems at the moment, beginning with the need to take a leak and that hankering for a smoke that seemed worse when there was a good reason not to light up. Longarm fished out a three-for-a-nickel cheroot and stuck it between his teeth unlit before he growled, "I told you before I could be wrong. The odds are better than fifty-fifty that the backshooting of Ferris Muldoon will remain unsolved. Officially, that is. When most everyone you ask suspects the same fired mine foreman as the killer, you worry less about who done it, and more about how to prove it in court. Foreman Pulver might have just been talking when he made those public threats. You go on home to supper if you're not as optimistic as this child, Sarge."

But Sergeant Nolan was a sergeant that balmly summer's eve because of an earlier occasion when Longarm had noticed something odd as he'd walked past the Tabor mansion on Capitol Hill, and had asked a copper badge with no stripes at all if he wanted to keep watch on an alley entrance. So the burly lawman in blue grinned wolfishly and replied, "That'll be the day. Herself is probably serving hash this evening after sending her dear relations home this morning so well fed at my expense. You told me what we were doing that time at the Tabors' grand house, with both the owners and their servants away to Leadville and all. I could see from the beginning why we ought to keep an eye on that furniture dray, and Silver Dollar Tabor in the flesh wrote a fine commendation for my saving of his fancy dinnerware from Paris, France. But I don't see what Thorpe Pulver could possibly be after in or about the grave of the man we suspect him of shooting in the back. I mean, what could the most black-hearted murtherer want with a man he'd already murthered? How many times would *you* want to shoot the same man in the same back?"

Longarm wearily replied, "I'll try to explain. Less than a full week ago Ferris Muldoon had a nasty public showdown with his mine foreman over by Lookout Mountain. None of the many witnesses can say what they were arguing

2

about, and our smooth-talking Thorpe Pulver keeps saying it was nothing. But at the time they had to be arguing about *something*. More than one witness has stated that when Muldoon told his foreman he was fired, Thorpe Pulver sneered that he'd have a better job to brag on when he dropped by to piss on his, Muldoon's, grave.''

Sergeant Nolan grimaced and said, ''I read thim same reports. But I took that last boast with a grain of salt.''

''Why?'' asked Longarm bleakly. He turned away and opened the front of his tobacco-tweed frock coat as he added, ''When you tell a man you mean to piss on his grave, and he's shot in the back and planted in his grave within the week, it's just possible you meant every word of your threat. I'm sorry, tree. I have to piss somewhere, and I ain't mad at anybody buried around here!''

As he watered the roots of a cottonwood in the deep shade of their chosen hiding place, Sergeant Nolan grimaced and said, ''*Aroo* and such a great one for hating deserves to study the rope dance no matter why he was fired! But what do you think they could have had such a falling-out over? Everyone who knew the both of them says they seemed the best of friends until that dreadful public shouting match on the streets of Golden Gulch. It's said Pulver was like a son to auld Muldoon and his wife. Ate supper with them every Sunday and often slept over. More like a relation than a hireling until that fateful Monday morning when the two of thim tore into one another out front on the street and all!''

Longarm buttoned his tweed pants and adjusted the ride of the cross-draw rig he packed his double-action Colt .44-40 in aboard his left hip and under his coat. Chewing the soggy end of his unlit cheroot only served to make him crave a deep drag more than ever. Off in the graveyard gloom a night bird trilled. So Longarm didn't answer Nolan. He nudged him to gain his attention as he placed a finger alongside his aquiline nose.

Nolan nodded silently. Despite spending most of his law-enforcement day patrolling the pavements of the mile-high

3

metropolis, Nolan had been raised country enough to know that night birds were more likely to be bitching about something than courting other night birds this late in the nesting season. So the two lawmen waited quietly, until they heard the crunch of shoe leather on gravel and spotted a dark figure moving their way between the tombstones in an oddly graceful way for a killer out to piss on his victim's grave.

"It's a woman," Nolan whispered, "and Jasus, for a moment I thought she might well be the banshee herself. Who could she be, out here alone at this hour with everyone gone and herself wearing widow's weeds?"

Longarm whispered, "The Widow Muldoon, of course. I recognize that fancy veiled hat with black satin roses, and I couldn't help admiring her figure in that tailored black bodice as they were lowering her husband's coffin just before sunset. Keep your voice down. I'm sure she wants to feel she's alone out yonder, whatever in blue blazes she may be up to out yonder."

Nolan suggested softly, "Maybe the poor woman only wants a private word or two with her dear departed. I was watching her during that funeral myself. Like a queen she carried herself, and sure, maybe she didn't want to say anything mushy in front of all thim others."

Longarm didn't answer. The mushy words of mourning widows made a man feel awkward. Besides, somebody else was coming their way through the seemingly deserted cemetery. As the figure made its way through the moonlit tombstones, they could see it was a man. Nolan murmured, "I could swear Thorpe Pulver was sporting a pearl derby like that one at the inquest. Jesus, Mary, and Joseph. You don't think he means to piss on a dead man's grave with his very widow looking on and all?"

Longarm quietly reached out to haul Nolan back as he murmured, "I somehow doubt the lady needs our help, Sarge. From where I'm standing, it looks as if the two of them were *expecting* to meet up there by that fresh grave!"

"And what if you're wrong? What if the murtherous fiend

came creeping through the twilight to desecrate his victim's grave, only to find his grieving widow out here alone and at his loathsome mercies?''

Longarm quietly pointed out, "She's not at his mercy. We're both within pistol range if he attacks her. Let's see if he attacks her before we get our bowels in an uproar.''

The tall thin figure wearing a fancy pearl derby did not attack the shapely form in widow's weeds. They greeted one another as old friends indeed, and melted into one another's arms above the grave of the late mining magnate Muldoon. As the two lawmen watched, they heard a girlish giggle, and it got tougher to make out the entwined mourning couple, if mourning was what they had in mind as they settled to the grassy mound above Muldoon's mortal remains.

Nolan gulped and whispered, "Bejasus and it sounds as if they could be rutting like hogs on the dear man's very grave!''

To which Longarm quietly replied, as he drew his .44-40, "Let's see exactly what Thorpe Pulver had in mind when he swore he'd piss on Ferris Muldoon's grave. Be careful. He seems to be a man who backs his brags, and those were .41 slugs and double-O shot the coroner dug out of Muldoon's spine. He could be packing a Le Mat Duplex.''

He was. Longarm eased in close enough to hear a gal sobbing for more and deeper, while a man's heavier breathing kept time with the wet smacks of bare flesh, until they suddenly stopped in what could have been the result of a mutual orgasm, or of that tanglefoot off to Longarm's left tripping over something between those other tombstones.

So Longarm was ready for anything as a pale moonlit figure rose like a bare-ass graveyard haunt with a massive ten-shooter gripped in both hands to throw down on the clumsy Sergeant Nolan!

Nolan fired wildly as Pulver discharged three rapid shots from his pistol wheel, while Longarm took aim, knowing the central shotgun barrel of a Le Mat could hardly miss a man-sized target at that range. So his two hundred grains of .44-40 lead socked Pulver in the jaw, busting it all to hell and sending splinters of lead and bone up through the bottom of his brainpan to drop him in his tracks.

As he flopped out of sight like a deflated balloon, the widow woman he'd been consoling bare-ass atop her husband's grave jumped to her own feet, stark naked in the moonlight, as she shrilled like a banshee of Nolan's old-country legends. But since she wasn't pointing guns at anyone as she wept and swore and pawed the air, they had no call to gun her as they moved in from either side to calm her down, or leastways get some duds and Nolan's handcuffs on her.

Longarm didn't want to make the arrest himself, seeing they'd be trying her in a local court. But as Nolan held her black skirts and bodice up to her, without much reaction on her part, Longarm felt the call to raise his voice above her mindless mewings and shout, "Stuff a sock in it and listen to me tight unless you want to hang by the neck until you are dead, you nastly little thing!"

Some of that seemed to sink in. She suddenly grabbed her bodice from Nolan and covered her moonlit tits as she sobbed, "Thank heaven you gentlemen got here in time! You saw how he was raping me atop my poor husband's coffin! He said if I failed to satisfy his vile lusts in every way, they'd find me out here just as dead come the cold gray dawn!"

Longarm said, "Yep. Like the French keep saying, *cher-chez la* two-faced *femme* when you want to know why two old pals suddenly get to hissing and spitting like tomcats on an alley fence!"

He glanced over at the sprawled naked body of the man she now aimed to betray in turn as he wearily told Nolan, "Let's get her dressed and cuffed before we see if she'd like to make a statement walking out to the road and our own hired buggy, Sarge."

Nolan knew his onions. He didn't argue as the two of them got her in shape to run on into town, with her blathering on and on about her poor dear husband trying to protect her from the advances of the fresh young mine foreman. When they had her ready to go, Nolan asked Longarm, "What about himself and that murtherous weapon he was packing?"

Longarm said, "I'd grab the Le Mat. It's likely the murder weapon. The rest of the evidence will keep until the morgue crew can get out here, Lord willing and the coyotes don't beat them to the smell of blood on the night air. We want to get this lady into the care of your police matrons as quick as possible."

Nolan didn't ask why, and they hustled the Widow Muldoon downtown to Police Headquarters while she babbled on and on about a mad mine foreman who'd raped her many times over in Golden Gulch, while her husband was away from the house.

As experienced lawmen, they knew she'd stick to that story and elaborate on it as long as she thought there was a chance in Hell of selling it.

They got her to repeat her grand notion about being saved from a homicidal rapist out at Cherry Hill Cemetery by Longarm and Nolan as they were booking her. It was only after she'd been booked, and was facing a mighty grim gray dawn after a night in a lonesome cell thinking it over, that she suddenly realized both Longarm and Nolan had taken turns at raping her, after they'd shot poor Mr. Pulver for reasons that still escaped her.

The district attorney just laughed when the suddenly rich young widow's expensive lawyer tossed that countercharge in front of the grand jury. The prosecutor had signed depositions from a booking sergeant, two matrons, and a couple of detectives on night call that the lady had told a very different story when first arrested on a charge of criminal conspiracy.

Over at the Denver Federal Building, Longarm's boss,

Marshal William Vail, agreed that the wild-talking widow had been lying to her husband, and no doubt her secret lover, about her plans for her old age. After her rich old husband had caught her fooling around and fired her younger stud, she'd talked the stud into gunning the poor old cuss before her husband could figure out how to rid himself of *her*.

As they talked it over in Billy Vail's oak-paneled office, Longarm allowed that the state of Colorado had more than enough to convict her and that he doubted they'd keep him tied up in court for more than a day or so.

The older, gruffer, and fatter Billy Vail scowled across a cluttered desk at his senior deputy and said, "You ride for the Justice Department. The taxpayers of These United States do not pay you to waste time in any local courts on local felonies, damn your eyes!"

Longarm shrugged as he sat across from Vail, and asked, "What was I supposed to do when Denver police seemed to be stuck? Let a killer ride off into the golden sunset with his victim's wife and mine holdings?"

Vail shook his bullet head. "You done what you had to do and I'm proud of you. Now I'm sending you the hell out of the state to help another old pal whilst they find that local bitch guilty without you! What's got into you, old son? Do you *enjoy* the hemming and hawing of courtroom proceedings all that much in high summer?"

To which Longarm could only reply. "Not hardly. Tell me where you're sending me and who you want this child to catch at what."

Chapter 2

It wasn't that easy. Longarm was still working on why they wanted a civilian lawman from such a distant court as he was changing trains in Cheyenne. He was traveling light, seeing that his orders were to report to the Provost Marshal of Utah Territory at Fort Douglas. Longarm more often toted his own McClellan army saddle along on a field mission to save wear and tear on borrowed horseflesh. But since he'd be issued any mount he needed by the army out yonder, they'd surely have lots of spare riding gear. Longarm liked to travel light for the same good reason he favored low-heeled boots with no spurs. When a lawman had to move suddenly, he had to be able to move suddenly. So as he boarded the westbound Union Pacific night flyer just as the sun was setting in Cheyenne, he was only carrying his Winchester '73 and twin saddlebags, cradled over his left forearm.

They allowed him six cents a mile traveling solo, and he liked to save as many pennies a mile as possible, considering his damned smokes cost him three-for-a-nickel. But there was a knack to riding free aboard the UP varnish, and the first rule was to let the conductor call the tune. Pilgrims who didn't travel much by rail tended to think that the white men who punched their tickets were one step above the colored porters. But in point of fact, the conductor was in command of the whole train and got to fire engineers who sassed him. So the conductor of a long-haul Pullman varnish expected to be treated with some respect, and not even President Rutherford B. Hayes in the flesh was about to ride this train over the South Pass Country by moonlight without a ticket or a gracious invite from its high-and-mighty ticket puncher.

Longarm had ridden that Burlington freight north from Denver for free, after bullshitting with a friendly brakeman he knew. He hadn't been able to find out whether any UP men he knew would be with the crew aboard this night flyer. So he took a south-facing seat in one of the cheaper coach cars, but rested his rifle and saddlebags on the hard wood seat to his right, prepared to pay if he had to and trying not to look as if he expected a softer ride at the expense of the UP stockholders. An earlier occupant of the same seat had cracked the grimy window open during the hot afternoon haul across the High Plains to the east. So Longarm was free to brace his left elbow on the sill, but he resisted the temptation to light up. There were ladies boarding among the other westbound passengers, and he knew they'd be asking for everyone seated by a window to shut it any time now. They didn't heat the cars in high summer, and they'd soon be tear-assing through thin bone-dry air that didn't hold heat worth mentioning at this altitude.

There seemed to be enough seats to go around as the warning bell began to toll up forward and a distant voice called "Booooard! All aboard!" So Longarm would have been mildly annoyed when a petite brunette in a rose-covered hat and a gray travel duster loomed above him as if she expected him to move his damned baggage out of the way of her derriere.

But that was a mighty shapely derriere, and the face that went with the silly hat was vapidly pretty. So Longarm ticked his hat brim to the lady and rose to heave his own load up atop the brass-railed baggage rack as he said, "Your servant, ma'am, and would your rather sit by the window?"

The young gal stared wildly down toward the fly of his tweed pants, or mayhaps his boots, as she asked, "Wasn't there a floral carpetbag on the floor near that window when you took my seat, good sir?"

To which Longarm could only reply, "I didn't know this was anyone's seat, ma'am. I saw no ticket stub stuck in that brass holder. You can see for yourself I don't have anyone's carpetbag on hand. Where might you have been while I was boarding this train just now?"

She blushed a becoming shade of dusky rose and looked away. Longarm knew better than to pursue the matter further. The sign on the ladies' room door distinctly asked passengers not to flush while the train was standing in the station, but when you had to go you had to go.

To break the awkward silence, Longarm asked if she'd left her stub as well as her overnight bag unguarded all that while. When she confessed she had, he sighed and said, "There you go then. Things could be worse. The one who lifted your baggage helped his or herself to your ticket. How far west were you going?"

She sobbed, "Virginia City, by coach from Reno! Whatever am I to do! I only have a few cents in the change purse in my pocket because they told me it was best to hide my traveling expenses in a change of stockings in my bag!"

Longarm told her, firmly but not unkindly, "They should have told a young lady who doesn't seem too well traveled, no offense, that you never part with anything valuable aboard a railroad train, whether it looks valuable or not."

The train started up with a jerk that inspired her to grab the back of the wooden seat, even as she wailed, "Oh, no! I have to get off! I don't have a ticket! I don't have any money! What if they make me get off out here in Indian country with night coming on?"

Longarm shut the window, rose, and stepped out into the aisle with her, saying, "First you sit and calm yourself a mite, ma'am. Before I pull the emergency cord, do you have anybody here in Cheyenne you could turn to for help?"

She said, "No. But I could wire home for money, collect, couldn't I?"

He sat down beside her. "You could. Then you'd get to wait around the depot Lord knows how long on seats no softer than this one. So listen to me tight before you make any more hasty plans. To begin with I am the law, federal. I am U.S. Deputy Marshal Custis Long, with the authority to arrest anybody committing the federal crime of robbing an interstate railroad train. This train will be stopping to jerk water more than once through the night. How do you like it so far, ma'am?"

She demurely replied, "I'm Roxanne Tremont. You may have heard of me. I'm a coloratura soprano. But I don't know what you're talking about, ah . . . Custis."

He explained, "They always take a few minutes to jerk water, and there's often a Western Union office close by. I'm sure of the one at Bitter Creek. There might be one closer. Either way, you can wire home or ahead and tell them to meet you with a money order when this train rolls into Ogden. You have to get off there and change to the Central Pacific line unless you're booked on transcontinental Pullman, see?"

She did. But she still looked confused, and asked about the thief grabbing her ticket stub as well.

He said, "Somebody boarding at Cheyenne just long enough to snatch a bag and jump back off would have had no call to steal *anyone's* stub. He, she, or it would have wanted a traveler from out of town to stay on board and get on out of town some more. The only call the thief would have had for stealing your ticket stub would be to ride on free, with no ticket of his or her own, at least as far as Ogden. See?"

This time she did. Her big brown eyes widened with worried hope as she lowered her voice and replied, "The thief must still be aboard this very train with us! He must still have my bag! All we have to do is tell the conductor and search everybody else's baggage, right?"

Longarm said, "Wrong. To begin with, no baggage thief with a lick of sense hangs on to a floral carpetbag longer than it might take to go through it and hide it somewhere. I'll be mighty surprised if we recover your stolen baggage in the same car as the thief. But it's a start. We'll talk to the conductor, and he'll have his crew of porters nose about in ways that might not be discreet for us to try. Porters are *supposed* to mess with baggage as they make up Pullman bunks or ask passengers to keep the floors of the cars clear."

She asked, "What if they threw my bag out a window back there?"

He said, "They could have. It would have been taking a needless risk. Folks notice floral carpetbags flying off trains in the sunset as they watch a train leave town. Be easier by far to just step into a secluded hideout, one of the johns or maybe a private compartment, and rifle the bag, wedge everything they don't want in any handy nook or cranny, and go on back to his or her coach seat. I say coach seat because any thief who'd already booked Pullman passage would have left your stub where you'd stuck it. You *do* have the *rest* of your ticket on you, don't you?"

She blushed again and confessed, "I had everything but my change purse in my bag. I know I was a blithering idiot *now*! But this is the first time I've ever had my baggage stolen!"

Longarm nodded soberly and said, "The first time is usually the most memorable, ma'am. Do you have any acting experience to go with that opera singing I should have known about?"

She sounded a tad lofty as she confided that all coloratura sopranos had to be able to "emote" on stage.

He said, "Swell. Just play along with me as I talk to the conductor, and if you don't make a liar out of me he won't catch me in any lies."

He didn't have time to explain in detail before, sure enough, a gruff old cuss Longarm had ridden with before came into their car to commence punching tickets and tear-ing off stubs for new passengers out of Cheyenne as he checked the seat stubs of those who'd been aboard to begin with. When he got to their seat Longarm said, "Howdy, Gus. I'd like you to meet Miss Roxanne, who's helping me with what seems to be a pattern of interstate larceny. We just now left a decoy carpetbag for the rascals to purloin, and they sure purloined it back there at the last stop."

The conductor glanced up at the baggage rack. Longarm said, "I held on to my Winchester, of course. They didn't nibble at the saddlebags you see. Miss Roxanne here can describe the fancier carpetbag they fell for."

Roxanne did, as old Gus took out a notepad and wrote down some of her details about red roses with purple leaves and stems against a field of lemon yellow. Longarm could almost picture the missing bag himself. But he'd already noticed she thought red roses had purple leaves to go with them, judging from her rose-covered hat of yellow straw. Women could sure go to a lot of trouble trying to match things that just didn't go together.

The conductor was so interested in catching thieves aboard his train that he never asked either one of them a thing about tickets. So Longarm pushed it further by confiding, "We might be able to work sneakier if we had us a private compartment to work out of, Gus. How much would it cost the government if you could see your way to that?"

The conductor said, "Nothing, if you'd care to wait till we get to Medicine Bow. A rich stockman and his wife will be getting off there in three or four hours, Lord willing and the Shoshone ain't out. Nobody else has booked their compartment for the night, and the porter made up their bunks with fresh linen this afternoon."

Longarm wondered exactly why the older railroading man had made that particular point. He'd introduced Roxanne as his sidekick, not a bedmate. But that was the infernal trouble with traveling anywhere with a female suspect or sidekick. Folks always figured you were out to screw them no matter what you said you were up to.

14

By this time it was almost dark outside, and Longarm suggested they go forward to the dining car, seeing that the early supper rush ought to be about over by then.

Roxanne didn't argue in front of the conductor. But as Longarm rose to herd her up the aisle, taking his rifle and saddlebags along, she seemed sort of pensive.

He didn't care. He hadn't lied outright to anybody, and he had to wonder if she could say the same. He'd known opera singers before, some in the Biblical sense, and all of them had traveled with opera troupes, often aboard private cars. Roxanne Tremont, if that was her name, was the first opera singer he'd ever met riding coach aboard a night train.

Out on the platform between cars she suddenly turned to him and bleated out, "I really *am* on my way to Virginia City to sing in *The Barber of Seville*. In the chorus, I confess. I'm really not an adventuress trying to play a fellow traveler for a free ride and my long-overdue supper!"

"The thought never crossed my mind." Longarm lied gallantly, as he shoved the door behind her open. "I'm hungry too. Ain't eaten since noon, and they serve fair grub aboard the UP varnish."

As he herded her on along a corridor past a row of compartments, he told her, "Most lines make you get off and snatch a warm meal now and again during a water stop. There's this Englishman named Harvey who's been making a fortune setting up trackside beaneries along lines that don't have Pullman's dining cars as yet. But I don't care to eat in a rush so I can run for my train. I like Mr. Pullman's roll-along restaurants better."

She said, "Listen, as soon as we get to Ogden I mean to pay you back for all these favors. In cash. That's all I ever repay my just debts to anyone with. Is that understood, kind sir?"

Longarm chuckled down at her and replied, "I hardly ever ask for a kiss with my dessert when I take a lady to supper, Miss Roxanne. If I took you for a gal in that line of work and I was willing to pay for such professional serv-

15

ices, I'd offer cash first and let you buy your *own* durned supper.''

She dimpled up at him and said she was glad they understood one another and that in that case she'd be pleased as punch to take him up on his kind offer.

Once they got forward to the dining car, and Longarm had chosen a table where he could sit with his back to a bulkhead and his Winchester across his thighs, he suggested the fried oysters with spuds and asparagus. She said that sounded swell, and remarked how she'd read in the *Rocky Mountain News* how Denver's answer to Wild Bill never sat with his back exposed if he could help it.

Longarm was too polite, and too smart, to ask how come an opera gal from back East had been reading the *Rocky Mountain News* about him just before she'd chosen the same seat that *he'd* then chosen. He didn't ask how come she'd chosen the name of a big Denver hotel as her stage name either. He knew he could ask Gus later whether anybody in the crew recalled her and that rose-covered hat from earlier in the day, or whether she'd boarded the train at Cheyenne as he had.

Either way, he could still hope she was no worse than a wandering flirt who felt no call to pay her own way in a world filled with poor wayfaring strangers of the male persuasion.

He hated to think anyone who could smile across a table at a man in such a friendly way could be out to do him *really* dirty.

On the other hand, he'd *been* done really dirty, by gals he'd been really dirty with. It hardly seemed fair. But a gal could hate you a lot and never let it show, with no soft cock to give her away.

Chapter 3

They got into Medicine Bow a little after ten that evening, where that rich old stockman and his pretty young wife got off, walking a tad stiff after all that time cooped up in private. By this time the porters had searched high and low for any carpetbag on board with as wild a floral pattern as Roxanne had described. Gus was of less help when it came to the pert brunette's trim figure and ridiculous hat. He said he'd relieved Pop Webber at Cheyenne, and just couldn't say whether Roxanne had boarded at Omaha as she claimed. They kept written records on compartments and Pullman seats that were made into bunk beds at night. They kept records of baggage checked through up forward. But Gus said they'd never had call to worry that much about unreserved coach-class seats or carry-on possibles.

Roxanne was in a dither about wiring home to Iowa for another loan from her dear old mom, since her dear old dad had about run out of any toleration he'd ever had for life upon the wicked stage. But they were pressed for time at Medicine Bow, and he assured her she could wire just as well from Rawlins, fifty miles west, before midnight. But she was one of those sweet little things with a whim of iron, and so they wound up having to run for it with the night flyer set to leave them stuck for the night in front of the

Western Union at one end of the Medicine Bow depot. She almost lost her hat, and she was laughing like hell by the time Longarm was hauling her back on board with her feet taking ten-yard strides through the empty darkness beyond the end of the platform.

Longarm sure hoped she was only playing him for travel treats. He was starting to like her despite the whoppers she kept trying to feed him.

Gus led them to the vacated compartment, where Longarm would at the least be able to store his own baggage safely. The conductor seemed to be mighty riled by the thought of a thief running loose aboard a train he was commanding. As Roxanne shucked her hat and travel duster inside the compartment, Gus took Longarm aside in the corridor to confide that he'd asked a couple of the porters about rose-covered hats and garish carpetbags to no avail.

Gus added, "They admitted they pay way more attention to the Pullman trade. Day-coach passengers ain't famous for handsome tips. One of my porters thinks he might have remarked on that outrageous hat boarding earlier today at Omaha. But he wasn't ready to swear it was Miss Roxanne, and none of the others recall her or that hat at all. What's all this bullshit about, Longarm? I know what you told me about somebody stealing her carpetbag. I know the two of you ran for the Western Union back there at Medicine Bow. Have you ever had the feeling you were missing something because somebody tore some pages out of the book?"

Longarm sighed and said, "I'm missing a mess of pages my ownself, Gus. Starting from the first page I've been allowed to read, my orders are to report to the provost marshal at Fort Douglas with a view to a delicate arrest. The military police ain't supposed to arrest civilians if they can get a deputy marshal to perform the chore."

Gus asked, "Don't they have a U.S. marshal's office attached to the federal district court in Salt Lake City?"

Longarm said, "They do. My own boss, Marshal Billy Vail, suspects we may owe this train ride to President Ruth-

18

erford B. Hayes and his advanced notions of appointments on merit. He's appointed a former Confederate official as postmaster general, and put a total Dutchman by the name of Carl Schurz in charge of Mister Lo, the Poor Indian. So the Texas Rangers who rode for the South are back in the saddle, and a whole slew of Saints have been appointed federal marshals out in Utah Territory since Hayes took over and made me wear this damned necktie on official business!''

Gus nodded soberly and said, "By Saints you mean Mormons. I know the proddy rascals think they're Latter-Day Saints. So you're saying the regular Christian military police sent for you to arrest some fool Mormon civilian, lest the Mormons raise hell with them for arresting a Mormon civilian, or tip that civilian off that he's about to be hauled before a federal court on . . . what?''

Longarm shrugged and said, "I don't know yet. You eat the apple one bite at a time and farther along, like the old church song goes, we'll know more about it and understand why. Have your porters looked through the trash bins for that missing carpetbag?''

The conductor said, "If they haven't they will. What's that got to do with your real reasons for riding this train out Utah way, old son?''

Longarm shrugged and said, "I don't know. I'd feel better about lots of things I've been told by the lady if I could be more certain she ever *had* a fool carpetbag. She did just wire someone in Sioux City described as her long-suffering mother. I've slowly managed to wriggle it out of her that she's not exactly a famous opera singer. She says she's had a heap of singing lessons and that a pal wired her there was a vacancy in the chorus for *The Barber of Seville* out Virginia City way.''

Gus asked if Longarm believed her.

Longarm shrugged and said, "I'd like to. I'm going to feel foolish if it turns out I've been feeling this sorry for a big fibber.''

Before the conductor could answer, they were joined by one of the white-jacketed Pullman porters who was proudly holding out a woman's carpetbag covered with as wild a floral design as Roxanne had described!

The porter said he'd found it under some bed linens when he commenced to break them out for the Pullman bunks the next car up. Longarm opened the bag to see it seemed full of ladies' notions, mentionable and not mentionable. He thanked the two of them and took the recovered bag in to Roxanne.

The petite brunette looked smaller but more shapely in her purple print summer frock as she perched atop the bedding of the narrow bunk that the previous lusty occupants hadn't asked to have converted back to facing seats. When she saw what Longarm was holding, she jumped up to grab for it like a drowning gal who'd just spied a floating hatch cover. She dropped back to the bedding with it to start pawing through the contents, squealing with delight as she pawed out one treasure after another to scatter across the bedding. Longarm watched, bemused, with his back leaning against the closed door.

He asked how come she'd been carrying those Western newspapers, such as the *Cheyenne Eagle* and *Rocky Mountain News*. She said she'd bought them aboard the train earlier from the candy butcher hawking apples, oranges, and peppermints.

Then she produced what seemed a wad of rolled-up black stockings and almost screamed, "I can't believe it! They never thought to look in here!"

She popped the roll open to spill a modest but hardly-to-be-laughed-off wad of bank and U.S. Treasury notes atop her other recovered treasures. Longarm said, "Congratulations. Your thief was in too much of a hurry to rob you right. He, she, or it just pawed through your stuff for money, jewels, watches, or whatever, and gave up early to stash the bag out of sight in such time as there was to work with. That ticket stub is the last chance we have. Do you have the longer ticket folder you bought in Omaha?"

She dug around, started to say no, then triumphantly produced what might have been taken for an unbound booklet threatening to fall apart all over the place. Longarm held out his hand for it as he told her he wanted to copy the number of her ticket for Gus the conductor. He was commencing to feel she really had to be a green train traveler when he had to tell her, "Each of these attached squares is good for a day's ride aboard the various trains you need to change to all the way out to Reno, where you have to start from scratch with the coach line south. The stubs torn off the larger tickets bear the same numbers. The whole idea is to save you passengers having to dig out your whole pile every time the conductor comes through after a stop. The thief who took your bag and seat stub is still using it, somewhere aboard this very train, as we waste time jawing about it!"

He half turned to duck back outside. Roxanne said, "Wait, don't go. Not just yet. We have so much to talk about now."

Longarm reflected that they were chugging through the night in the middle of nowhere with Rawlins over an hour off as he sat down beside her and asked what she wanted to talk about. It might have been taken the wrong way if he'd asked for some straight answers for a change.

She said, "Now that I have my money back, I have to wire my poor old mother before she sends me that money order in care of the Ogden Western Union."

Longarm nodded and said, "That's easy. We'll be stopping to jerk water before midnight. Have your message composed in advance this time, and we can get it off from Rawlins so's your folks will have your second wire before they can get to their bank in the cold gray dawn."

That reminded him of an old practical joke, and he had to chuckle. So she naturally asked him what was so funny.

He said, "I just thought of this Texas gal I know who likes to play practical jokes on pompous folks, state senators and such. She sends them a telegram timed to arrive after

21

midnight and instructing them to disregard the previous message. It gets funnier as you study on it, picturing the pompous old bird you've woke up with *one* telegram trying to get back to sleep as he wonders what that *other* one might have said.''

Roxanne made a wry face and sniffed. ''I don't think that's funny. It sounds mean, if you ask me. Was she pretty, this Texas gal with such a droll sense of humor?''

A true answer would have been needlessly cruel. So could the brassy Texas blonde in question, come to study on it. He said, ''We won't send any comical telegrams to Sioux City. You're still going to want to make sure when you get to Ogden, though. If your wires have crossed and they sent you more than you need, you can just wire a money order back from Utah. Or better yet, once you get to Virginia City and make sure you have that job. It's been my sad experience that you never have too much pocket jingle as you travel through this land of woe and scandalous prices on or about railroad property!''

She said, ''You've saved my having to buy another ticket, and I must say this bunk bed is a lot more comfortable than that bench back in the coach car. But you have to let me pay you for the supper I was forced to let you buy me, Custis!''

Longarm laughed and said, ''I'm making three or four cents travel expenses every minute even as we speak. We've both ridden free all the way from Cheyenne, and I might still show a net profit from the time we dallied in the forward dining car.''

She firmly lined three quarters up on the blanket between them as she insisted, ''I was paying attention to the prices on that menu, and I knew all that time you thought I was one of those hussies who romance strangers on a train for their own travel expenses, or perhaps a little net profit. That was why I warned you before you bought my supper that I wasn't willing to play that game.''

She lowered her lashes and looked away as she added,

"It wasn't easy. I hadn't had a bite all afternoon and I was awfully hungry."

Longarm scooped the six bits up and put them in his pants pocket as he rose to peel off his frock coat, hat, and gun rig, hanging the .44-40 handy to the head of the bunk on a bulkhead hook. He saw she'd draped her duster and perched her hat over the fold-down commode near the built-in corner sink. She likely hadn't known that the innocent-looking low-slung wooden chest opened up as a handy shitter with a view of the cross-ties whipping past below when you pulled the chain to flush the simple plumbing mechanism. That was why they asked you not to flush the toilets when the train was standing in a station.

Longarm hung Roxanne's hat and duster up without saying why. As he sat back down beside her she demurely remarked, "I can see that other couple never turned down these covers after this bunk was remade for the day. I hope that conductor was right about them using fresh linen. I'd feel all icky sliding between used sheets some total strangers had been . . . intimate on. Wouldn't you?"

Longarm gulped and replied, "If that's an invite, we'll be getting off at Ogden just after breakfast time up forward. Once we do, I'll be boarding a southbound local and you'll be transferring to the Central Pacific line. Before we get to such sweet sorrow, I thought you told me you weren't that sort of a gal."

She met his eyes again, sending smoke signals with her own as she replied in that logical voice females use on re-tarded children, or on any man who can't read minds, "I'm *not* that kind of a girl. That kind of a girl makes love for money. We've just established that I don't *owe* you any money. So can't we start from scratch as . . . fellow travelers?"

Longarm reached out to haul her in. But just before they kissed he felt obliged to warn her, "I mean what I said about us having to part, however friendly, in the cold gray dawn."

To which she demurely replied, "Don't be silly. This

23

train won't make it to Ogden before eight or nine. I asked. So we'll have more than time enough for . . . breakfast."

So Longarm lowered her to the covers and proceeded to explore her with his free hand while she explored his tonsils with her tongue, and a good deal of huffing and puffing could be heard through the compartment door as a slender slinky stranger dressed like an undertaker held his ear to the thin wood paneling outside.

But then the gruff gray conductor was grumping along the corridor, and the man who'd been eavesdropping on Longarm and Roxanne rolled his back to the bulkhead to go through the motions of fishing for a smoke.

Old Gus shot a thoughtful look at the passenger in fusty black as he approached. He recognized the passenger lurking in a Pullman corridor as one of the coach car riders and said so, demanding to know what the cuss was doing this far forward.

The man in black gripped the derringer in the side pocket of his frock coat as he smiled as sincerely as he knew how and said he'd just felt like stretching his legs and mayhaps grabbing a smoke up forward where it wouldn't offend the ladies in his own car.

Gus said, "There's two smoking cars. One at each end of the coach-car section. Go thou and sin no more where you don't belong as you smoke yourself blue in the face for all I care. But move your seat stub with you. I know I'm being an old fuss, but we'll have others getting on at Rawlins, Bitter Creek, and such as the night wears on."

So the hired killer allowed he'd do that, and never drew on old Gus as he drifted back where he belonged for now. The conductor he'd been about to gun had given him a swell suggestion. With any luck at all, the lawman he'd been hired to kill could wind up bare-ass and sound asleep by the time they'd be stopping where a man could just kick in a flimsy door, shoot the both of them, and drop off to hole up in the dark until he could steal a horse and ride off laughing.

Chapter 4

The UP tracks ran almost due west past Medicine Bow. So
while the rolling sea of shortgrass lay silvery in the bright
moonlight off to the north, it was black as the pit in their
compartment once they'd trimmed the oil lamp. But Roxanne still insisted on leaving her corset and black lisle stockings on, along with her high-button shoes. She was afraid
they've have a train wreck and others might see her stark
naked. Longarm didn't want to upset her by pointing out
she'd look just as bawdy with her bare tits and ass hanging
out either end of her laced-up stays. The pink corset gave
him a good grip on her trim waistline when they got around
to trying it dog-style, and when she confessed a hankering
to get on top, Longarm was able to help her bounce when
he hooked his fingers under the bottom edge of her figure-
enhancer.

From time to time their train made a turn and allowed
moonlight to stream in the usually north-facing window.
When it did, Roxanne covered her perky bare nipples with
her hands and begged him not to peek as she went right on
sliding up and down his Maypole. She said that she couldn't
understand what had her so excited between her thighs that
evening. Longarm had made love in the South Pass Country
before, and a sawbones back in Denver had explained the

25

effects of high-altitude fornication to him. But he didn't think it would sound romantic to tell a gal what was going on as they were both trying to come again.

To the casual eye the moonlit scenery whipping past outside was just more of the same Wyoming prairie off to the east. But the tracks were crossing over the Continental Divide and the buried spine of the Rocky Mountains where there'd been less upheaval but just about as much in the way of uplift. They were rolling along and screwing like mink high in the sky, where the thin air seemed to make gals lightheaded and willing, even while it made men work harder to satisfy the sweet little things.

But Longarm was more used to high-altitude screwing than most, since he was based in the mile-high city of Denver to begin with. So when Roxanne just couldn't keep going on top, he gallantly rolled her over on her back and finished right with her high-button shoes crossed around the nape of his neck.

As they drifted back to the real world, Roxanne said, "That was just lovely. How soon will we get into Rawlins, darling?"

Longarm blinked, kissed her with his old organ-grinder still inside her, and decided, "Ten or twenty minutes. Are you saying you want me to take it out?"

She sighed and said, "Just long enough for me to send that wire to my poor little mother, dear. She's going to be worried enough by the first wire as it is, and we can do this all we want as soon as we've relieved her mind, see?"

He did. He'd always been fond of his own little mother. It was easy for him to just roll off and reach for his duds. As he did so he told her he'd be proud to hop off, send her wire, and hop back on without her having to get out of bed and dress up.

But she said that there was plenty of time for her to get dressed and she was looking forward to him undressing her again. So when their night flyer hissed to a stop in Rawlins, the two of them were on the platform at the far end of their

Pullman car. It was smarter to get there first because lots of other passengers dropped off at such stops to stretch their legs and gape about, whether there was any good call to or not.

There were some new passengers and their baggage waiting at the only railroad stop for miles. So despite the hour, when you added in the passengers from their train, there was some clutter and confusion on the Rawlins platform. So Longarm took the lead and bulled on through to the Western Union shed down by the end, and got Roxanne to composing her latest message home on a yellow telegram pad. They had a good six or eight minutes, thanks to those crewmen unloading some big and bulky cargo from the baggage car behind the tender. So Longarm resisted a serious urge to warn the dutiful daughter not to explain more than she had to.

Roxanne finished her message and handed it over the counter to the night clerk. But before they could settle up, all hell seemed to break loose outside.

Longarm snapped, "Stay put and keep your head down!" as he turned toward the rapid-fire rattle of gunfire with his own gun already drawn.

He stepped out on the platform just as a spidery figure in fusty black dropped off the rear steps of that same Pullman car with a big Schofield .45 in each hand. As the two-gun man shoved a passenger gal on her ass to tear Longarm's way along the platform, the experienced lawman had the time to reflect on why so many train robbers favored quick-loading Schofields. So when he yelled, "Stop in the name of the law!" and the wild-eyed stranger threw down on him with his own guns, Longarm simply fired first. Both those army-issue .45s went off in his general direction as his more tightly aimed .44 slug punched the man in black in the breastbone and off his feet.

Longarm advanced cautiously. He could see the one he'd just shot was out of the game. But it had been Cole Younger *and* Frank *and* Jesse James who'd stopped the famous Glendale Train. So Longarm was covering the dark slot at the head of the railcar stairs when old Gus dropped out into the light along the platform to take in the scene at a glance and call out, "Praise the Lord! I thought they just killed you and that Miss Roxanne! They kicked in your compartment door and shot the liver and lights out of the bedding along the window. Feathers and gunsmoke still fill the air inside. Who in blue blazes *was* he?"

Longarm began to reload as he soberly suggested, "Same cuss who got on with us at Cheyenne, lifted a lady's carpetbag and her seat stub, and took another seat, waiting for a chance such as he just took."

Gus came over, stared down in the tricky light, and declared, "I did see this bird lurking outside that compartment not more than an hour ago. You say he was out to steal Miss Roxanne's baggage?"

The lady they were talking about was coming their way through the crowd now, despite what Longarm had told her. Longarm told the older man, "He didn't bother to go through her carpetbag before he cached it in the first linen locker he passed. It was her ticket stub he was after. He wanted us all to think it had been filched along with her carelessly left bag by a sneak thief. He had the fare for a train ride over the Divide. He just didn't want any ticket clerk recalling that ugly hatchet face, and he knew every ticket agent would be questioned once he'd killed me."

A younger man dressed more like a cowhand, with a pewter badge to back his own two six-guns, had pushed through the crowd to join them just as Longarm accused the dead man at his feet of murderous intent.

The night deputy patrolling Rawlins alone on such a normally quiet time knew Longarm on sight from earlier railroad stops and that Indian scare they'd had with Buffalo Horn and his Bannock a spell back. So he only echoed the conductor's question as to who they were talking about, and added, "How come you're so sure he was after *you*, Longarm?"

The more experienced lawman said, "My boss, Marshal Vail, describes it as the process of eliminating. When I got on that train back in Cheyenne, I was naturally looking for a seat near the bulkhead at one end of the car or the other. Anyone else who's spent any time studying gunfights would have already considered scouting such seats. When he scouted Miss Roxanne's and saw she'd left the very seat stub he wanted for his ownself, he snatched up her bag, grabbed the stub, and lit out to leave that same seat as a logical place for me to fort up. Unlike Gus here, I don't recall him from the train. He must have been trying to keep me from seeing him. I enjoy a rep for remembering faces. I wish I could place this one. I don't. He was needlessly cautious until he figured this stop would be a good place to make his move."

The town law chuckled fondly down at the sprawled cadaver and said, "You surely proved him wrong. I know you're the law and all, Longarm. But the coroner of Carbon County is still going to want a deposition from you about this shooting."

Gus grumbled, "He ain't got time! I got a timetable to meet and this train is supposed to get to Bitter Creek just after midnight!"

Before any argument could get going, Longarm said soothingly, "Just toss my baggage off and I'll be proud to catch another train, Gus. My own office is going to want a full report and, if possible, the identity of this misguided soul. I don't see how I could manage all that aboard your night flyer, no offense."

Roxanne tugged at his sleeve to whisper that she was staying there too. Longarm took her to one side and whispered back, "Honey, I had more than one sweet position I was saving up for the western slope. But we have to think practical. I'm going to spend half this night talking to other lawmen and sending wires to even others. All that while the whole county seat is going to be staring a heap and gossiping more. They ain't had this much excitement in these parts

29

since the army caught up with old Buffalo Horn. I know this because I was scouting for them up this way at the time. So in all modesty, I'm well known here in Rawlins, and we were going to part discreetly when we got to Ogden in any case."

"But Custis . . ." she began. Then old Gus was shouting for everybody to get on board, and Longarm gently but firmly got her on board, swapping her shapely form for his saddlebags and Winchester as the train gave a jolt and one of the porters had to grab hold of Roxanne to steady her.

Longarm dropped off the now-moving steps as the confounded gal called something mushy after him. Longarm walked back to where a much thinner crowd of pure locals still stood around the total stranger he'd lain low. He saw somebody had picked up those two Schofields. He mentioned them casually to the night deputy. The Rawlins lawman said to call him Dave, and allowed that the guns had been impounded as evidence. Longarm had no use for a brace of horse pistols anyhow.

Someone had gone to tell the county coroner about the reasons for so much noise in such a small town at that hour. So a meat wagon came by to carry the remains over to the undertaking parlor cum county morgue, and Longarm sent some wires as young Dave stood by to watch how it was done.

Once they were free to repair to the taproom of the only hotel worth mentioning at that altitude, Dave ordered them a pitcher of beer and a corner table where others could only pester them from two sides. A red-nosed newspaper stringer who usually served as one of the town drunks had already been chased away twice because Longarm was not in the habit of bragging in print when he had no idea what he had to brag about yet.

He felt it was safe to confide in his fellow lawman Dave that he figured he was the intended target of that attack on an empty Pullman berth for two reasons.

He said, "*Numero uno*, the young lady I'd just escorted

over to your Western Union was an aspiring opera singer from Iowa, and I'd be surprised as hell to discover she has any connections with anybody out in Utah Territory, where she's never been before. Second, I *am* on my way to Fort Douglas to make a serious federal arrest somewhere in Utah Territory. I don't know much more than that. But I was told it was a delicate matter, and my boss and me took that to mean the provost marshal has some call not to ask for help from any closer federal lawmen affiliated with the Church of Jesus Christ of Latter-Day Saints.''

Dave whistled softly. "You reckon that jasper we have on ice across town this evening could be one of them Mormon gunmen they call their Destroying Angels?''

Longarm shrugged and said, "I've been assured by members of the Mormon Temple in Salt Lake City that the Danites, as they were called by their own kith and kin, were disbanded by the late Brother Brigham after some of them got out of hand.''

Dave said, "I've heard some of them Damn-knights were still out busting windows and burning barns when folks forgot to pay their church tithes. Some say the killing never stopped when the army hung Brother Lee for his part in the Mountain Meadows massacre.''

Longarm sipped some beer, fished for a cheroot he'd be free to smoke at last, and said, "Elder John D. Lee was never a Danite, as far as any outsiders could tell. He was assigned as an Indian missionary, and he seems to have got all mixed up when the Paiute tangled with a wagon train down Mountain Meadows way. Some say the Mormons told the Indians to attack. Others say a wagon master called Fancher was spoiling for a fight. Either way, the fight was a mean one, with a score of emigrants down and most of their stock rode off with before Elder Lee and some Mormon militia rode in. Lee always said he'd meant to escort the shot-up survivors to safety, but some of them turned mean and taunted his white riders into turning on them. Some kids too young for the Mormons to gun down beside

31

their parents later claimed Lee and his riders had started shooting the men, women, and older children they'd disarmed just to satisfy the Indians. In any case, the army hung John Lee within sight of whatever happened. The Salt Lake Temple allowed they'd never ordered him to gun anybody, red or white. They disavowed some *other* fanatic elders I tangled with over to the Great Salt Desert. Once you get some old boys cranked up with rifles and revelations, it can be a chore to calm them down again."

He got his cheroot going good and added, "Speaking of calming down, I'd best see the night clerk next door about hiring myself a bed for the night. I want to get an early start at wrapping things up here lest I miss that *day* train to Ogden!"

So as Longarm was getting a room for the night up in the South Pass Country, two other men were getting a room in another hotel that overlooked the union yards in Ogden.

They called one another Pat and Mike because those were not their real names. As the one called Pat tipped the bellboy, locked the hall door, and doused the bed lamp, the one called Mike moved over to the window with a tall bull-fiddle case. He opened it to take out a Springfield .45-70 fitted with a telescope sight. He raised the window blind, stared down at the lamplit loading platforms behind the big brick depot, and chortled, "Perfect. Me and old Widow Maker have a field of fire covering anybody getting off the UP from the east or out to board that spur line south to Fort Douglas by way of Salt Lake City."

His sidekick growled, "Stay away from that open window with that rifle gun until we see that train roll in come morning. We're being paid to see *him* before he sees *us* and they say he's a sharp-eyed son of a bitch!"

The man gloating by the window snorted, "Don't be such a worried soul. Old Longarm has no call to suspect anybody's after him, and he's miles from here right now in any case. The poor nosy bastard."

Chapter 5

Longarm wasn't the only one wiring far and wide for some answers after he failed to get off the UP night flyer in Ogden the next morning. The gunslicks laying for him across from the Ogden depot with a scope-sighted army rifle sent their own wires, and were advised their target could have simply missed connections in Cheyenne, and were ordered to wait for the UP *day* flyer, due to arrive before sundown.

Nobody anywhere seemed able to shed any light on the true name of the man Longarm had shot in Rawlins. Dave Craig, the town law showing Longarm around, insisted that the funereal garb of the dead man made him a likely Danite. But Longarm was the only one there when they got around to an autopsy the next morning who knew about the peculiar underwear conservative Mormons wore. Male and female Saints wore the same white cotton union suit, with squares cut out of the crotch and for each nipple so they could function modestly in the eyes of man as required by natural needs or desires.

The son of a bitch on the zinc slab had been sporting red long underwear under his black serge suit and *buscadero* gunbelt. He had no tattoos and no serious scars. His vaccination mark might have meant he'd served in the Union Army. He looked to be about the right age, in his middle

33

thirties, for a vet. On the other hand he could have just had careful parents. Halfway educated folks who could afford it had been having their kids immunized against smallpox with a dose of harmless cowpox since old Tom Jefferson had been president.

The closest thing to identification found on the mysterious corpse had been a library card from Cheyenne, applied for and issued the morning Longarm had boarded the Burlington local for Cheyenne. Dave opined, and Longarm agreed, that a cuss too shy to buy his own coach-car tickets would want some identification on him that wouldn't tell the law half the truth about him. Longarm was more worried about the obviously phoney name the rascal had chosen for his library card. Nobody thought for a minute he'd been named Bart Windsor. But there was a Windsor Hotel as well as a Tremont Hotel in Denver, and Longarm had as much as shoved Roxanne aboard that night flyer against her will.

But on reflection over breakfast, Longarm remembered Roxanne telling him she'd chosen her stage name after the fancy Tremont neighborhood of Boston town, and of course nobody in Denver had invented the name of that fancy Windsor Castle where Queen Victoria entertained in style. So it was likely, or at least possible, that he was stringing some unrelated events into a diabolical pattern nobody had ever planned. A man tracking stock over slickrock or trying to put together a puzzle had to watch out for seeing patterns where no patterns really were. A gal aspiring to sing opera, a man out to hide his true name, and somebody whipping up a fancy name for a hotel in any town were as likely to pick Buckingham, Montclaire, Tremont, or Windsor as any other. It was true Roxanne had gotten to that particular seat ahead of him, or said she had. But if she'd been lying just for Longarm's benefit, that porter never would have been able to recover her missing baggage. The man who called himself Bart Windsor *had* been carrying the stub she claimed to be missing, and he'd surely shot the hell out of a compartment she'd been sharing with the intended target, so how could they have been working together?

Longarm still sent a wire to Virginia City. He felt a lot better about the pretty little thing two hours later, when an opera house man he knew from that tour he'd taken as a bodyguard to the Divine Sarah Bernhardt wired back that they did indeed have a Miss Roxanne Tremont on their list of performers.

By noon Longarm had decided he'd try some mountain oysters fried with onions as he read through the latest batch of wires. Billy Vail was having a fit in Denver over the tedious trip Longarm was making out of getting to dammit Fort Douglas, not the Presidio of San Francisco for Gawd's sake. Marshal Fred White from Tombstone had wired that a gunslick answering to "Bart Windsor's" general description had left town earlier that spring after gunning a miner in Lou Rickabaugh's Oriental Saloon. The miner had been fired from the Tough Nut as a suspected high-grader. It was unclear whether the gunslick known in Tombstone as Bart Strand had been hired to gun a thief, or had gunned a fellow thief over the profits they'd agreed to split.

Old Fred's observation that the first name was a tad unusual tended to single out a hatchet-faced cuss who favored a black suit and a brace of .45 Schofields. But Longarm warned himself not to bet all his chips on another lawman's educated guess. He had a local photographer shoot a death portrait of the Bart Windsor on hand so he could send it to Tombstone and have them compare it with their own Bart Strand. If the two were one, he added up to a paid assassin. If they weren't, he wouldn't. You ate an apple a bite at a time and didn't swallow before you'd chewed.

The coroner's inquest was cut and dried, but took longer than a man in a hurry had to spare. By the time Carbon County had decided that a paid-up lawman on a mission had every right in the world to shoot a mysterious stranger out to kill him, that westbound UP varnish he'd been planning to board had come and gone.

But there was more than one way to skin a cat or get to

35

Utah Territory. Longarm ambled over to the rail siding with his Winchester and saddlebags. He only had to hand out a few three-for-a-nickel cheroots before they told him a low-ball rattler would be coming through in less than an hour. When it did, Longarm bummed a ride in the caboose for a slow but sure trip over the submerged spine of the continent.

As most everyone knew, a train rolling "highball" had the right of way, and "lowball" freights and other trains got shunted off on sidings to clear the single track between stops and let the more profitable highballing trains keep rolling. The rattler Longarm was riding that afternoon was slowly hauling half a mile of empty reefers back to the Ogden yards. So it got to stand on sidings a lot, and seldom rolled more than twelve miles an hour the rest of the time.

Looking on the bright side, he was riding free with a friendly crew in a comfortable caboose with unlimited coffee, and he still figured to beat the next night train down the western slope, if not by one hell of a lot.

They'd crossed the upper Green River before sundown, and were steaming over the Wasatch Range even more slowly, about the time the next night flyer he could have caught would be leaving Cheyenne. He had no way of knowing how tired Pat and Mike had gotten of waiting for him by that time. He was pleased to be making such good time the hard way. They picked up speed, more speed than they really needed, on the steeper grade west of the rail cut over the last serious mountains. Longarm offered to help, but the brakemen told him not to be silly, so he got to sip coffee alone for quite a spell as the brake crew managed, with some effort, to keep the long rattler on the track going a mile or more a minute.

The engine crew knew that section as well as their onions. So they let her coast far and fast along the flat stretch between the mountains and the railroad town of Ogden.

They were still doing better then their usual twelve miles an hour as some of Longarm's brakeman pals rejoined him and they began to pass lamplit windows on either side in the balmy summer darkness. Everyone had seen that famous photograph of the official "Wedding of the Rails" shot in 1869 at Promontory, not Promontory *Point,* just north of the Great Salt Lake. But in point of fact, that had turned out to be a poor place for two big terminal yards and a transcontinental junction. So the Central Pacific and Union Pacific had agreed to swap passengers and freight at the more logical location of Ogden, east of the lake on flat as well as solid ground.

You had to stand back a piece from the Great Salt Lake. Its level varied considerably from one spring thaw to another, and the lakeshores sloped so gently that a rise of a few feet out in the middle of the lake could spread the briny margins a few miles.

The vast rail yards at Ogden stood high and dry a dozen miles from the usual shoreline of the lake and a prim walk from the Mormon town founded on the Ogden River back in '51 by Brother Brigham. The Gentile railroading settlement that had filled in the space between the yards and the more neatly laid-out parts where you couldn't order liquor, tobacco, or coffee was still run as naturally as any other Western town of the era. The Mormon elders officially in charge were willing to live and let live where there was so much profit to be made, as long as it was understood that nobody whistled at a gal or fell down drunk more than a block or so away from railroad property.

Longarm didn't want to whistle at any gal or fall down drunk as he parted friendly with his railroading pals and cut across the freight yards with his saddlebags and Winchester. He'd asked the railroaders, so he knew he'd missed the Salt Lake City local sent north to meet up with that UP varnish he'd failed to board in Rawlins. There would be a later local. But he was mighty tired of train riding, and wasn't sure they wanted him to turn up at Fort Douglas after they'd blown Taps in any case. So once he made it out to the paved street that ran on past the depot, Longarm headed for a fair hotel he knew of old down the other end of the street.

Nobody was watching with a Springfield .45-70 as he crossed over to approach the front entrance. Nobody was expecting him at that hour.

There was nobody laying for him in the dark dinky lobby. He hired a room upstairs for a dollar, and asked if the kitchen was still open behind the adjoining hotel restaurant. The room clerk said he might still make it if he hurried. So Longarm took the stairs two at a time, locked his possibles away in the room right next to that booked by Pat and Mike, and hurried downstairs to grab some warm grub. His bowels were really growling after all that weak coffee he'd been swilling since noon.

He didn't want to have to scout up another place to order steak and potatoes if he could help it. So Longarm strode into the almost empty hotel restaurant in a determined way that could have been misread for intent—and was, as one of the two sedately dressed gents supping at a corner table across the room gasped as if he'd been stung by a bee and rose to crab sideways and slap leather, shouting, "Great day in the morning! It's *him*! He's *tricked* us!"

Longarm had no idea who they were or what they were so upset about. But when two grown men were drawing on you, it was usually best to aim at the least hysterical one first. So the hired gun called Pat caught Longarm's first round just over the heart and bounced off the floral wallpaper behind him to slide down out of sight, leaving an ugly red smear across lavender carnations, as Longarm swung the muzzle of his six-gun through its own smoke to cover the second man.

But he held his fire as the one called Mike let his own side arm fall and grabbed for the pressed-tin ceiling, shouting, "I give! I give! I give!"

A cook ran out from the kitchen with a cleaver in answer to the banshee wails of the waitress, who was cowering under a far table with some other late patrons. Longarm snapped, "I'm the law. Federal. Go get me some *local* law. What are you waiting for, a kiss good-bye?"

38

The cook ran on through the archway to the hotel lobby as Longarm moved in on that corner table. He told the one he was covering to step away from the revolver he'd dropped. As the ashen-faced gunslick did so, Longarm stepped closer to kick the man's Manhattan .36 conversion along the baseboard as he cast a glance behind their table at the one he'd shot.

That one had drawn a Colt Lightning .38. He was still gripping it. Longarm didn't care. Nobody had ever looked that dead without being completely sincere about his feelings. A corpse sure bled a lot on its left side after two hundred grains of hot lead had torn through that big artery atop the heart muscles.

Smiling thinly at the one who'd given up, and who seemed to be wetting his wool pants, Longarm told him not unkindly, "We'll let you lower those hands behind you, in cuffs, as soon as that cook gets back here with some backing. I could see by your outfits that neither of you herded cows for a living as a rule. Those small-caliber guns add up to discreet shooting at close quarters, along with a certain self-confidence in your marksmanship. But no offense, I've never seen either of your faces before. So let's start with who the hell you are and who the hell you're working for."

Mike tried, "We weren't working for nobody. What's this all about? Me and poor Pat were just having our supper at that table in the corner when you came in and threw down on us with your own cruel six-gun!"

Longarm said, "That ain't going to work. Before you dig yourself in any deeper, I'd best advise you that whether you two gents are Saints or not, I'm on friendly terms with the local law, Mormon or Gentile. I was through a spell back bodyguarding the Divine Sarah, and got them all free tickets to her show."

As if to prove him right, an older gent with a familiar face as well as a German silver badge came in from the lobby with that cook and some other locals holding drawn guns. The Mormon deputy nodded at Longarm and said, "I might have known it was you, Uncle Sam. Who's that you seem to be holding at gunpoint this evening?''

Longarm said, ''I'm still working on that. His pal lies behind that corner table with the supper plates atop it. I was only after my own steak and potatoes when the two of them slapped leather on me.''

The Mormon lawman stepped over to the corner table and dryly said, ''That was mighty foolish of them. You say you don't know who they are or why they were gunning for you?''

Longarm shook his head and waved his gun muzzle at the one he'd taken alive, saying, ''This natural survivor was about to tell us. Who are you and what's this all about, you heroic cuss?''

But by this time some color had returned to the gunslick's face, and whether he had the balls for a fair gunfight or not, he had the jailhouse shrewdness to know nobody was going to gun him or even treat him really mean in front of so many witnesses.

So he almost sneered as he replied, ''My name is Mike Smith. This inhuman monster just shot my partner, Pat Jones. The two of us were on our way east after the California mines we worked for shut down. We naturally had to go for our own guns when this homicidal maniac came in here and started up with us for no reason.''

One of the onlookers from the lobby next door allowed that the two of them had gotten a room upstairs the night before. The Mormon deputy asked the name of that California mine they'd worked for.

Longarm said, ''Save your breath. He's a hired gun and he's wanted somewhere for a hanging offense.''

The older lawman asked, ''You mean you've recognized him?''

To which Longarm grimly replied, ''I recognize the pattern. You can see, I can see, and he can see I've got him and his late pal on attempted murder minimum. So he'd be offering us a deal if there was any deal he could make. The only outlaw who can't hope for a reduced sentence in exchange for some sweet singing is an outlaw wanted on a charge that just can't be reduced. Let's cuff him and go up for a look through the room they hired. Don't need a search warrant, unless the hotel manager here objects.''

Chapter 6

The manager was dying to see what had been inside that bull-fiddle case the strangers had come in with. So they all went upstairs, and when the surviving gunslick allowed he'd misplaced his key, the manager opened the door next to Longarm's with his passkey.

There was nothing in the bull-fiddle case on the bed. The man who wanted to be called Mike Smith said he'd been robbed. Longarm picked up the scope-sighted Springfield .45-70 someone had propped in one corner near the window and decided, "This looks enough like a stolen army rifle to hold him on suspicion until the army says it ain't."

Mike Smith snarled that he'd never seen that rifle before, and cussed them for trying to frame him and that traveling companion he'd barely known before Longarm had gunned him for some reason.

The accused federal deputy stepped over to the window with the Springfield and trained it out and down to peer through the scoped sight before he decided, "They were fixing to nail somebody changing from the cross-country to the Salt Lake City line. I wonder who it could have been."

The Mormon lawman said he felt sure their prisoner would want to tell him after a private discussion of the matter in a back room at the city jail.

Longarm grimaced and said, "Let's just hold him on mopery and see who comes forward with a writ of habeas corpus. It's tougher for a lawyer to fake his name in front of an honest magistrate, and it makes more sense to see if we can find out who they were working for than it does to beat a sensible story out of a suspect. A man can get convincing as all get-out with a split lip. But we'd still have no more than his word until we can corral him closer to somebody we know better."

The town law agreed that made sense, but asked, "What's mopery? I don't recall that charge on the municipal statutes or even from the Book of Mormon."

Longarm smiled thinly and said, "I ain't sure there's any law agin it, but there might be and we ought to be able to hold him on it until a lawyer comes forward to object. Different jurisdictions define the offense of mopery in different ways. Denver would have it that a suspect with no visible means who seems to be just loitering around and moping silent and sullen might be up to most anything."

So they marched Mike Smith off to jail as a mysterious mope, and put Pat Jones on ice at the county morgue for the night.

Longarm knew better than to prowl a town as prim as Ogden for pussy when at least two hired guns had been waiting there to back the play of that other one back in Rawlins. But it sure was tough to fall asleep with a hardon and a worried mind. He couldn't even make an educated guess at who might be trying to stop him from doing what before he got to Fort Douglas and found out what the War Department wanted him to do for them.

That was easier said than done. In the morning he had to call on both the county coroner and Billy Vail's opposite number in Ogden, a Mormon elder cum U.S. marshal named Reynolds, to explain, or try to explain.

That wasn't easy either. The county coroner was willing to settle for depositions from Longarm and his half-dozen witnesses that those total strangers had commenced an un-

43

provoked gunfight with a U.S. deputy marshal on a mission. But neither the marshal nor the coroner was as happy when Longarm told them, truthfully, that he didn't know any more than that about his mission.

The older and more astute U.S. marshal of the Mormon persuasion was less mystified. He and Longarm had worked together before, and before that, the distinguished Marshal Reynolds had taken part in the earlier "Mormon War" with the U.S. Army—on the Mormon side, of course.

When Longarm truthfully told him he thought the provost marshal at Fort Douglas wanted some Gentile arrested and whisked out of the Utah Territory before the papers got wind of it, the gray-haired Reynolds made a wry face and said, "We heard they'd been having a really serious desertion problem out our way. With the price of beef rising and other jobs in mining and railroading opening up, a lot of immigrant boys who signed up in desperation seem to be having second thoughts about that thirteen dollars a month."

Longarm scowled across the desk, wishing it was Billy Vail's so he could smoke, and replied, "This child is not about to round up army deserters. That ain't my job. It aint your job either, no offense. If it was, I fail to see why they'd want me to come all the way over here to do it for you. There's nothing all that political in any lawman of any persuasion holding a deserter long enough for his own military police to pick him up."

Reynolds said, "It's an election year. The opposition papers have been having a field day with what they call the overly tolerant ways of President Hayes and Interior Secretary Schurz when it comes to us wild Indians, unreconstructed Rebels, and religious fanatics."

Longarm snorted, "Shoot, they won't serve hard liquor at a formal White House supper, thanks to the tolerance of Miss Lemonade Lucy. Old Rutherford has just been using common sense about treating folks he'd licked with common courtesy. Mexico might still own Texas if old Santa Anna had appointed Davy Crockett the Mex Alcalde of San

44

Antone after eveyone had calmed down. Texas Rangers who rode with Hood against the Union are still good Texas Rangers, and you Saints who've been out here in the Great Basin over thirty years have to know the country better than anybody else old Hayes could pick.''

Reynolds looked past Longarm with a thin smile as he said, half to himself, ''We should have held out longer. That scheming Buchanan only appointed a Gentile governor and sent troops to depose our own Brigham Young in '57 as a distraction, and the War Between the States broke out just as the Salt Lake Temple accepted a compromise. There were forty thousand of us and only twenty-five hundred soldiers. We won most of our dustups with them, and had Washington really worried, when they used the war back East as an excuse to leave us alone.''

Longarm had heard similar sad tales from Red Cloud of the Lakota Nation and many a trail herder who'd once owned a vast plantation on the Virginia Tidewater, or so he'd said. So he told the proud old veteran of past glories he was sorry as hell the Republic of Deseret had wound up as Utah Territory, and allowed he had to get on down to Fort Douglas, where a U.S. Army had reined in before they could finish off such a peculiar bunch.

Marshal Reynolds walked him out front, where they shook and would have just parted friendly if Longarm hadn't thought of something else.

He said, ''Over in Rawlins more than one Gentile lawman thought that mysterious Bart Windsor I shot on the railroad platform fit their own notion of a Danite, no offense.''

The older man, who'd spent more time as a Mormon elder than a U.S. marshal, looked pained and said, ''I wish the newspapers would stick to the man-eating plant of Madagascar or the Loch Ness monster when they have a slow day. When Brigham Young was interviewed by Horace Greeley, he admitted to seventeen wives at the time and denied ever hearing the term Danite or organizing any Destroying Angels. That madwoman who tours back East, claiming to have escaped from Brother Brigham's harem, seems to be the source of a lot of such nonsense."

Longarm nodded soberly and said, "I know you Saints and the men of Wyoming have shocked the blue blazes out of your women by allowing them to vote. But I did save some unwilling gals from some Destroying or Avenging Angels out on the Great Salt Desert a spell back. I was told at the time your Salt Lake City Temple hadn't sanctioned such behavior."

The Mormon lawman nodded curtly and almost snapped, "You were told the simple truth. We were told when our leaders signed that peace treaty with Washington that a Saint must obey the law of the land."

Longarm didn't say anything.

The older man smiled sheepishly and continued. "All right. Some of our brothers and sisters still practice polygamy. You just pointed out that our women have more rights than some, and what would you have an old man with two old wives do at this late date, throw one out in the cold?"

Longarm grimaced and said, "I've had this conversation before, and I don't lose any sleep over the private lives of otherwise honest men. I'm talking about them killers I've run into personally rightly or wrongly described as Destroying Angels of the Church of Jesus Christ of Latter-Day Saints."

The marshal shook his head, but allowed, "You could have run into fanatics from other claimants to the Book of Mormon. *We* are the only *true* followers of the Prophet Joseph, of course. When he and his brother were murdered by a mob in Illinois, an emergency meeting was held to appoint a Council of Twelve Apostles headed by Brigham Young. But there were dissenters who didn't come West at all, or broke off with the Council of Twelve after they got this far. There are over a hundred congregations back East who describe themselves as a Reorganized Church of Jesus Christ of Latter-Day Saints, with their main temple in the town of Independence, Missouri. There are other splinter sects known mostly to themselves as Temple Lot, Bickertonites, Cutlerites, Stranites, and so forth. But all that guff about Destroying Angels is still guff. Nobody blames the Church of Rome when an Irish tenant burns a haystack, do they?"

Longarm smiled thinly and replied, "As a matter of fact, some English landlords have. But nobody's sent me into Fenian country to arrest a soul. So I'd best get on down to Fort Douglas and see who they *do* want arrested."

That was easier said than done. The morning was nearly used up by the time he got himself and his possibles down to Salt Lake City and wrangled a ride out to Fort Douglas aboard an army mail ambulance.

The differences between an army outpost, a camp, or a fort had to do with the size of their garrisons. You hardly ever saw built-up fortified defenses around anything bigger than an outpost, manned by little more than a patrolling squadron. Mister Lo, the Poor Indian, was seldom dumb enough to attack the full regiment based at what the army called a camp and just ran a fence around. Fort Douglas had started as Camp Douglas, about three miles northeast of the Salt Lake Temple. But now it was a corps headquarters west of the Rockies, with more going on than you'd find camped with your average regiment. So it got to be a fort, and they seemed to think an interior guard mount was enough to discourage attacks by local Indians, Saints, or both.

He'd been told Major Preston Sullivan, an old pal of Billy Vail's, was the provost marshal who'd requested a hand. So he was puzzled and chagrined when he was shown into a spartan office where an older rusty-haired gent with gilt leaves on his army blues stared up at him as if he'd just seen a haunt and gasped, "Jesus H. Christ! It's *you* again! I asked Billy Vail to send me a good tracker!"

Longarm saw nobody was inviting him to sit down. So he invited his own weary rump to settle into the wicker chair on his side of the desk as he modestly replied, "He did. If I ain't good enough I'll just go on back to Denver and you can go on and fuck yourself. I know I got here later than

47

you'd expected. Somebody tried to stop me at Rawlins. When that didn't work, they tried again at Ogden. The three losers answered to Bart Windsor, Pat Jones, and Mike Smith. I took Smith alive. They're holding him for me up Ogden way. Do you want him, and how come you have such a hard-on for my fair white body?''

Major Sullivan said, "None of those names ring any bells. They're all yours. I have enough on my plate, and I was still an MP captain that evening you knocked my superior, Lieutenant Colonel Walthers, ass-over-tea-kettle along that railroad siding. Does that ring a bell for you, or do you just have some grudge against this man's army?"

Longarm sighed and said, "I tried sincerely to work with that total asshole. Have you ever caught yourself talking to somebody after they were out of the room? Talking to officers and gentlemen as stupid as Colonel Walthers leaves me feeling just as dumb. So might anybody be home under that red hair, or might I be speaking into a dead line on one of them newfangled Bell telephone sets?"

Major Sullivan smiled despite himself and grudgingly confessed he'd had his own dumb conversations with Lieutenant Colonel Walthers.

Then he suggested, "Let's start from scratch. That wasn't *my* jaw you dislocated. So I'll allow I might have been a tad out of line if you'd care to go back over what took you so long to get here."

Longarm offered a more detailed account of both gunfights, and tossed in what Marshal Reynolds had volunteered about Danites.

Major Sullivan said, "We don't tell them everything either. Do I have to explain what a military post this size is doing this close to their Salt Lake Temple?"

Longarm said he'd been told Washington made the Mormons nervous as well.

The major opened a desk drawer to take out some charge sheets and a sepia-tone photographic print as he growled, "We *want* them to stay nervous. We dasn't show them we're not in full control out here, and so we wash our own linen without their snide help!''

He handed over the typed-up onionskins and thicker photograph as he continued. ''In more realistic colors the hair might really be honey blond. The references on file at Personnel are certainly phoney.''

Longarm stared down in dismay at the portrait of a severely pretty young woman in a modest pleated bodice, with that light hair piled atop her fine-boned skull in a prim bun, as the provost marshal continued. ''Miss Zenobia Lowell, if that's her name, was hired to come out here and teach army brats their three R's. There was nothing in her contract about sex orgies or human sacrifice. So for openers, she's been charged with murder, arson, and theft of government property. We're working on some more delicate morals charges. That's where you come in.''

Longarm protested, ''The hell you say! You can't expect me to chase after another female suspect whilst I'm still under a cloud for that unchaperoned arrest of the Widow Muldoon!''

Major Sullivan insisted, ''We can. You have to. We've been assured you know this Mormon Delta better than any other lawman who's not a Mormon. We don't just *suspect* Zenobia Lowell of corrupting a bunch of her older students and having them murder the young girl who was trying to expose them. The poor kid got a letter off to the Inspector General before they tied her up and burned her alive.''

As Longarm stared thunderstruck, the provost marshal told him, ''I don't see how you'd be able to compromise yourself arresting our wicked schoolmarm *alone,* Deputy Long. When last seen, shooting her way off the post, she was leading a good-sized gang of army brats and deserters who've been gang-fucking her well ahead of you!''

49

Chapter 7

Neither red nor white human trackers tracked the way a bloodhound did. They couldn't follow a trail of footprints with their noses to the dirt, and even if they'd been able to, that wouldn't have been the fastest way to travel. A human tracker made up for his weaker sense of smell with a better brain than any bloodhound ever born. Unlike a sniffing tail-wagger, an experienced scout or lawman tried to guess the way his quarry was headed by the little sign it might have left.

It could be tough to scan photographs or read letters with a three-for-a-nickel cheroot gripped between one's teeth. So Longarm got rid of his smoke after Major Sullivan handed over a second photograph and the typed transcription of a formal letter to the Inspector General's Office back East.

The studio portrait was that of a pretty little brunette of sixteen or so. She'd still had some filling out to do, but she'd already looked more like a natural woman than the severe Zenobia Lowell. Her name had been Petula Dorman, and she'd dwelt at Number Nineteen, Officer's Row, if the opening paragraph of her military form letter was to be believed.

When Longarm commented on how she wrote like a typical army brat, the provost marshal shook his head and said, "I suppose you could have called the poor kid an army brat.

But she wasn't an officer's daughter. She was one of the children of our post sutler and his wife. They had to live on post instead of the nearest town because the nearest town would be Salt Lake City and they were Temple Lot Mormons."

Longarm almost said something dumb before he got his Saints sorted out in his head. Then he softly whistled. The Church of Christ (Temple Lot) were Mormons who'd begun by rejecting the leadership of Brigham Young to stay back in Missouri under Joseph Smith Junior, the son of the prophet, as members of the Reorganized Church of Jesus Christ of Latter-Day Saints. Only then they'd gotten into a fuss with Joseph Smith Junior over who owned the vacant lot indicated by the Lord as the site of a temple meant to form the core of a New Jerusalem.

Longarm confided to the Irish-American officer, "I understand the two sects are still fighting it out in the courts back East. I ain't too sure why, but I can see why a member in good standing of the Temple Lotters might feel unwelcome in Salt Lake City. They'd have had to pay rent to the army for quarters on Officer's Row, right?"

Major Sullivan sniffed and said, "Just as married officers have to. I take it you were an enlisted man when you learned so much about this man's army?"

Longarm said, "Don't get your bowels in an uproar. They taught us in this man's army that officers have to pay for their fancy duds, exclusive clubs, better grub, and nicer quarters out of their own pockets. That's likely why they get paid more than thirteen dollars a month and all the beans they can eat. Let me read the gal's letter through before we worry about where she was living when she wrote it!"

He did, and the late Petula Dorman had gotten right to the point in her formal opening, which read, "Subject: Crimes Against Nature Taking Place On Or About This Military Reservation."

Longarm glanced up to ask, "How did you all come by

this letter if that wicked schoolmarm or even one of her followers intercepted it?''

The officer grimly replied, ''They obviously didn't. IGHQ got it, sent a transcript to the Post IG, and demanded a full report. But by then it was too late for poor little Petula. They'd already killed her, burned down the schoolhouse, helped themselves to the garrison war chest, and ridden off on some of our best cavalry mounts. Read the damned letter before you pester me with questions that have their own obvious answers. Can't you see she must have sent another letter while they took their usual six weeks to reply to her through channels? One of the troopers who deserted along with Zenobia Lowell and her star pupils was assigned to that mail ambulance you rode out from town. Need one really say more?''

Longarm muttered, ''Not hardly,'' and read on. As he did so, he could see that this earlier letter that had gotten through only scratched the surface, although things were already getting pungent enough for a full IG inspection.

The young gal writing it had been the only female pupil in a sort of select postgraduate course Zenobia Lowell had been offering after the regular school hours.

Like most small schools set up for a few children of a good many ages, the one Zenobia Lowell had been hired to run at Fort Douglas had taught the elementary grades from first to eighth in one big room, with the two dozen kids of different ages and grades being taught in small bunches while the others worked at their desks on instructions the same schoolmarm had given them earlier. Longarm had found it confounding as well as tedious when he'd been a schoolboy back in West-by-God-Virginia. But he'd learned his three R's, sort of, so the system had to be better than total ignorance.

They had no higher school at Fort Douglas, so army families wanting kids to go on to high school and college had to send them on into Salt Lake City or beyond. But from what the one older female pupil had sent to IGHQ in stilted but no uncertain terms, their new schoolmarm had offered evening classes in what had been described as advanced *comme il faut* to polish up their social manners. Aside from the one gal in her teens, the course had included three older boys and that many younger enlisted men from the garrison who'd signed up for some classes they'd missed by dropping out of school earlier. The advanced course in sophisticated ways had been held in the basement of the post schoolhouse. That had made the late Petula Dorman uneasy to begin with. Then their sophisticated schoolmarm had handed out copies of two "adult" books and told them their assignment was to read them both and then write out book reports, deciding which of the two was the most wicked.

Longarm glanced up to say, "I could have passed that test without straining my brain. But where in thunder would they have managed to buy fifteen copies each of *The Unhappy Valley* by Richard Burton and *Justine* by the Marquis de Sade."

Major Sullivan said, "I've no idea, and I'm ashamed to confess it never occurred to us to look for any copies, now that you mention it! Are you familiar with either work?"

Longarm smiled sheepishly and admitted, "I've been known to read a book about beekeeping when I had nothing better to take to bed with me in a strange town. Where our wicked schoolmarm could have come by so many copies of either book is what we call in my outfit a lead worth following. Neither one is sold openly back in Denver. So there has to be an even more limited number of bookstores to study on in Salt Lake City. Richard Burton himself described it as the *City of the Saints* in another book he wrote about our own West. Burton is this English explorer and travel writer who surely likes to keep an open mind as he traipses about. So a heap of his books have to be sold in secret."

He thought back to that time when a copy of *The Unhappy Valley* he'd been reading in San Antone had inspired him to go back down to the Plaza Grande and pick up those

53

two frisky *señoritas*. He sighed and said, "Burton's guide-book only offers suggestions to a contortionist lucky enough to find himself the owner of an A'rab harem. A man would have to contort like hell to pleasure more than two or three gals at a time. But that's as wicked as *that* book gets."

He grimaced in distaste and added, "De Sade wound up in a lunatic asylum, and for all the pissing and moaning about free speech, I have to allow that's where he belonged. I mean, sticking your toes up a couple of gals' twats whilst another blows French tunes on your old organ-grinder may look silly as all get-out, but nobody winds up needing a doctor."

He shook his head wearily and continued. "*Justine* is old de Sade's admiring account of a nasty young gal who sets out to behave depraved and attains her goals with room to spare."

Sullivan smiled uncertainly and asked, "Then the correct answer to our wicked schoolmarm's required book reports would be that *Justine* is the wickedest work?"

Longarm shrugged and said, "It would have been if her dirty mind is playing with a full deck. There's this scene in *Justine* where the heroine, or villainess, has her own gang kidnap her own mother and tie her up helpless for Justine to get at. So Justine gets at her with a big fake prick strapped on so's she can rape her own mother up the ass with it."

The officer looked shocked.

Longarm said, "Me too. Justine's brag is that she's com-miting the offenses of incest, lesbianism, rape, and sodomy at the same time. But I can't for the life of me see how either woman would get one lick of sexual pleasure out of such disrespectful behavior. Old de Sade wound up in that asylum after he'd tortured a house servant with a razor and hot wax. He *belonged* in an asylum. The gal had been will-ing to screw him when she took off her duds for him."

He read on to where Petula Dorman only charged she *suspected* their depraved Miss Zenobia of more advanced lessons, given to some of the boys, before he nodded soberly and decided, "They must have caught her trying to send a more detailed report. They forced her to tell them, or mayhaps they just guessed, that she'd sent this earlier letter. Exactly what happened then?"

Major Sullivan wearily replied, "If only we knew all the details. We had no idea anything was about to happen the night it happened. IGHQ hadn't taken any action on that letter you're holding when the schoolhouse down at the far end of the parade burst into flames in the middle of the night. They'd tied poor little Petula to a post in the cellar before they'd set the place on fire. You could hear her screaming from amid the flames as the post engineers tried to get to her in vain. We think they doused everything with coal oil before they struck a light and ran. It was meant to draw everyone on post to that end of the parade, and it did. So we don't know too much about the way they opened the safe at Post Headquarters to grab the war chest. But we know they did."

Longarm knew the term, "war chest" stood for the slush funds kept on hand to pay for things such as emergency supplies that might not wait on the usual government paperwork. He asked how much they'd gotten and how they'd gotten it past the interior guard, or sentry, posted to watch over such post installations as supply dumps, stables, and such.

Major Sullivan said, "Eighteen hundred dollars. They shot him. He wasn't expecting real trouble. He only knew he'd better be able to report such a large group entering the stable compound after dark when and if the Officer of the Day asked him to repeat his first general order."

Thinking back to some nights when he'd stood his own tour on Interior Guard, long ago and far away, Longarm wisfully intoned, "I shall walk my post in a military manner, keeping always on the alert and observing all that takes place on or near my post."

The major said, "The blonde he'd already recognized as a civilian employee who belonged on the post was the one

55

who shot him. We expect him to live. But he's still very upset about that. I can't say I blame him. How would you like to be standing there with a single-shot .45-70 at port arms, asking a pretty girl a simple question, when she suddenly whips out a derringer and shoots you?''

Longarm said, "I'd doubtless feel hurt. Where'd she hit him?"

The provost marshal looked blank, then said, "Shoulder. The right one, I think. Does it matter? I told you we expect him to pull through."

Longarm said, "Everything matters when you're trying to picture just what happened. Sometimes a witness who's confounded, or lying, tells you things without picturing them himself. You'd be surprised how many liars I've caught because I just couldn't picture things happening the way they'd described them as happening. I'll want to talk to others on or about this post as well before I go tear-assing out across the Great Basin after a picture I ain't finished drawing in my head as yet."

The provost marshal tried not to let his impatience show as he asked Longarm how many others they might be talking about.

When Longarm told him he fumed. "Damn it, Deputy Long, it's likely to take you all day to interview that many witnesses, and you're not going to get all that much out of any of them! We've already gone over the whole case with everyone on the post, and naturally, hardly any of them were able to help at all!"

Longarm shrugged and said, "I only need help from one or two. You say a wicked schoolmarm I've never met and a bunch of schoolboys I have no names on ran off with her, six blank faces and the garrison war chest bound for parts unknown? This post is snuggled against the foothills of a considerable mountain range, facing a good-sized city, hundred of square miles of cultivated land, and a desert that runs all the way west to the Sierra Nevada. What were you expecting me to do before I questioned anybody, put my

56

head to the ground like that old Indian scout in that old joke?''

Major Sullivan said he hadn't heard any jokes about old Indian scouts with their heads to the ground.

Longarm looked disgusted and said, "I keep forgetting they give an officer a degree in *engineering* when they let him out of West Point. I never graduated from West Point. So I'll tell you a joke all the scouts without engineering diplomas know about reading trail sign."

Major Sullivan shot an annoyed glance at the clock on one wall as Longarm leaned back in his chair to begin. "Once upon a time these old riders come upon an Indian scout they know, flat on the trail with one ear to the ground. So they naturally ask him what's up, and the Indian tells 'em there's a buckboard about a mile down the trail, drawn by two mules and driven by a skinny Mexican with a big fat wife. That sounds reasonable until the Indian says there's two little kids, a puppy dog, and a cord of firewood in the wagon bed. When the Indian says the puppy dog is brown and the little gal has red ribbons in her hair, one of the riders asks him how in thunder he can tell all that from just holding one ear to the ground. The answer, of course, is that the fool Mexicans and their damned buckboard just ran over him and he's been trying to get back up ever since.''

Major Sullivan stared soberly at Longarm and demanded, "Is that supposed to prove some point, Deputy Long?"

To which Longarm could only reply, "That trooper they shot down like a dog got to *see* what was running over him. It's a lot tougher to form as clear a picture just from listening. But when listening is all I have to go by, I mean to ask a heap of questions. So what are you waiting for? Do you think I have all day?"

Chapter 8

First things coming first, they ate their noon dinner across the way at the officer's mess. It cost Longarm two bits, but the pork and fried spuds with asparagus was served on china, and both the coffee and peach cobbler dessert he washed down with it were tolerable.

He was glad he'd eaten first when they traipsed over to the post hospital to interview the civilian surgeon and the big ash-blond nurse who'd helped with the autopsy of Petula Dorman. The young gal who'd been burned alive had been boxed in a lead-lined coffin and shipped on back to Independence by that time. But they'd naturally taken pictures, and the nurse had typed up all the grisly details.

Longarm was just as glad the set of photographic plates had printed plain black-and-white. The contorted naked body atop the zinc table still looked toasted. The hair was all burnt off, of course, and the poor gal's tits looked more like marshmallows held over the embers way too long. The flames had licked at her face long after she'd just stopped screaming. So when Longarm held up that sepia-tone of the same gal taken in life, the resemblance wasn't all that striking and he said so.

The skinny gray-haired surgeon shrugged and said, ''You can see she'd filled out a bit since that portrait photograph was taken a year or so ago. But that was still Petula Dorman we examined in the basement. We had the advantage of having known her in life. I bought my cigars and medicinal whiskey over at her father's shop. Hiram Dorman was our post sutler, you know.''

"Was?'' asked Longarm. He didn't have to ask what a sutler was, having spent some time on army posts.

The surgeon's husky but not-bad-looking nurse explained, "Most of the family went East with the body for the funeral. But they'll surely be back in a month or less. They left two of their hired girls to run the business while they were gone.''

Longarm didn't want to cuss in front of a lady. So he didn't say a word about important witnesses not being around when you wanted to ask important questions.

He asked the medical team if it was safe to assume the body had been sealed in lead under a closed coffin lid *before* it had been released to the family.

The surgeon said, "Of course it was. The odor was enough to knock you off your feet, even after a rubdown and such embalming as we managed with so many capillaries open to the air despite the crust. I served in the war, and Nurse Ericsson here has helped out during more than one Indian scare since coming West. We still found the autopsy a rough time, and nobody but the father really wanted to look at the remains.''

"Did you let him?'' Longarm asked.

The surgeon said, "Of course not. It was his own daughter twisted and charred almost beyond recognition, and I still have bad dreams about total strangers I had to examine years ago after a forest fire swept the battlefield during the Wilderness campaign.''

He stared off into space and licked his lips as if he felt the need for some of that medicinal whiskey as he added, "They wanted us to see if we could tell how many of them had been dead by the time the flames swept over them. We could. I've never understood just why the army thought that really mattered. Lord knows we never put anything about that, either way, on the death notices we sent to their families.''

"How do you tell?'' asked Longarm, ignoring the warning look Nurse Ericsson shot at him. Her elderly boss looked as if he was fixing to cry as he found another photograph, a grimmer view from directly overhead, and said, "When you burn a dead body there's no smoke in the lungs before the fire reaches them. When you die in a fire you suck smoke and flame into your lungs until you just can't scream anymore. I was down there by the schoolhouse while she was still screaming. But see for yourself if you won't take my word for it!''

Longarm swallowed hard and looked away from the black-and-white view of charred lung tissue in an opened-up rib cage with a well-toasted tit to either side. As if to punish him for asking so many questions, the older man said, "You're not the first one to raise the stupid question of the poor child's identity. She died a virgin. Would you like to see a close-up of *those* charred organs? Are you really dumb enough to think a wicked schoolgirl led an attack on a virgin schoolmarm? That blond she-devil who burned this child alive shot a soldier who knew her on sight at point-blank range, and who are you to question my authority?''

Longarm modestly replied, "Just a lawman trying to do his job. Who else asked the same stupid questions about the dead gal, Doc?''

The surgeon swore and stormed out of the room without answering. Major Sullivan, standing in the other doorway, said, "I can answer that. Post Operations raised the possibility that the civilian they hired might not have been as wicked as the rest of us believe her to be. They don't seem to have any answer to the obvious questions that stick out like sore thumbs as soon as you even consider Zenobia Lowell as the victim.''

Longarm made a wry face and said, "I follow your drift.

But try her this way. What if a wicked schoolgirl wrote a lying letter about a schoolmarm she and her wicked playmates meant to murder and leave in her place?''

Major Sullivan snapped, "Don't be an ass. We all heard poor little Petula Dorman screaming her last, and you just heard the surgeon tell us the body they examined was that of an innocent virgin!"

Longarm shrugged and pointed out, "Schoolmarms older than Zenobia Lowell have been known to die old maids, and it's agreed the gang's *victim* wouldn't have been as wicked as the female who'd started all those evening orgies. I sure wish that body was still handy so I could get a better look at it."

Nurse Ericsson sniffed and said, "*We* got a better look at the poor child than we ever asked for. Dr. Sloan knew her personally. Don't tell him I told you. But he was crying by the time we'd finished that autopsy!"

Major Sullivan had started thinking harder since Longarm had begun to prod his brain for him. He said, "Aside from being less likely as an innocent young thing, Zenobia Lowell has turned out to be a proven liar about *other* things. The teaching college in Boston she claimed as her alma mater never heard of her. The references she presented when she applied for her job with Post Operations were deliberate forgeries, and that takes us back to it being *her,* not one of her pupils, male or female, who volunteered to hold those evening classes in the cellar, featuring literature you just can't find in any respectable library or on top of the counter in any cigar store!"

Longarm nodded thoughtfully, but said, "We only have the word of that one letter to the IG that any such books were ever handed out. My boss back in Denver calls what I'm doing the process of eliminating. It's all too easy to pile on more sign than there really is. So I try to brush away as many lizard tracks and tumbleweed scuffs as I can whenever I'm trying to track a fox over broken ground cover. I'll allow that letter to the IG and those fake references look bad for Miss Zenobia, if you want to concede we don't have another witness we can talk to about all those morals charges.''

Sullivan blurted out, ''I was about to take you into the ward next door to meet that interior guard Zenobia Lowell shot!''

Longarm allowed that sounded sensible. But in point of fact it was Nurse Ericsson who led the way to the modest eight-bed lying-in ward next door.

A ward attendant in white fatigues was playing rummy for match-stem stakes on one bed with the only two patients on tap that afternoon. The hospitalized troopers both wore army-blue convalescent robes. But only the younger one had an arm in a sling as they waited out any infection.

All three enlisted men popped to their feet at the sight of Major Sullivan. But the officer gave them an ''At ease,'' which still left the three of them on their feet, of course.

The wounded trooper, Glover, who'd been on Interior Guard the night in question gave much the same story Longarm had already been told. So Longarm started asking questions.

When he asked why Glover had challenged anyone who belonged on the post to begin with, the trooper repeated the general orders he'd been given at Guard Mount, the formation men detailed to the chore stood a few minutes after the post flag was lowered for Retreat. He added that Taps had blown and somebody was ringing the fire triangle as the seven of them came running toward the stables he was guarding after dark.

Longarm said, ''Don't get ahead of me and this pencil stub. The moon was full the night before last. So we're talking about a waxing gibbous moon last week. Did you have any lamplight or, say, a bull's-eye lantern to work with, soldier?''

When Glover said there'd been moonlight enough and moonlight alone, Longarm said, ''I read the statement the Officer of the Day took down at the time. I ain't doubting anybody's word. But I like to get a sharp picture in my head and I see some blurs. I know you'd just been shot and couldn't have been feeling too bright when they first asked you what happened. So let's start over. You're walking your post in that military manner, keeping always on the alert, and then what was the first unusual thing you noticed on or about your post?''

Glover said, "I told you, sir. They'd blown Taps, the moon was high, and I'd been walking that tour for a little over an hour when I heard the fire alarm. I peered about to see what might be burning. I couldn't see the schoolhouse from where I was posted. But I saw this orange glow down that way and then I saw that schoolmarm, three troopers I knew on sight, and those schoolboys I didn't know as well. They were running my way fast. I dropped my Springfield off my shoulder to port arms and called out the regulation challenge. I'd just yelled "Halt!" and never got to "Who goes there?" when that blond she-devil shot me, and the next thing I knew they were patching me up next door and the OD was there taking down the little I could tell him.''

Longarm frowned thoughtfully and decided, "That couldn't have been as much as I just read in the official report, no offense. Try to picture the bunch of them just as you got shot. Were those troopers wearing their dress blues or fatigues? What were those boys wearing? How about Miss Zenobia and how do you know it was really Miss Zenobia?''

Glover looked befuddled as he replied, "The schoolmarm had on this dark riding habit with no hat. That's how I could see right off it was her. The moon was shining on her pinned-up yaller hair. All six of the men with her were dressed for riding in civilian cow duds.''

Longarm glanced at Nurse Ericsson as he pointed out, "Miss Zenobia Lowell was hardly the only blond woman on or about Fort Douglas, and you say her companions were dressed as trail herders, meaning broad-brimmed hats that surely shaded their faces a heap in tricky light?''

Trooper Glover blinked at the nearby blond nurse and stammered, "Aw, you must be joshing me, sir. Nurse Ericsson never shot me with that derringer. None of the other blond ladies posted here were missing in the roll call the OD held before dawn! All the military personnel were present or accounted for, save for Troopers Weems, Klein, and Tim Garner. Tim and me bunked in the same barracks, and you get so's you can tell who's there by *any* light once you know a man that well."

"How do you know you were shot with a derringer? Did you really see such a weapon in anybody's hand, or did you just see a flash and feel a mule kicking you? I've been shot. So I know how confusing it feels."

Glover looked away as he muttered, "Must have been a derringer. They dug a derringer bullet out of me, didn't they?"

Longarm glanced at the nurse, who calmly replied, "Caliber .32. Low velocity. You're right about Trooper Glover being in a state of shock. The bullet severed an artery before his right scapula stopped it. But those deserters ran off with their army-issue Schofield .45s, so . . ."

"So naughty schoolboys could have been packing *any* caliber, and I've seen sissy revolvers chambered with nine rounds of .22. So the question before the house is how much this injured youth remembers and how many words might have been put in his mouth."

Glover protested, "I ain't lying or even shaving the truth, sir! I've no call to cover up for any durned deserters who'd leave a comrade in arms bleeding in the moonlight like a stuck pig!"

Longarm said soothingly, "I ain't accusing anybody here of anything, old son. I've written down guesses of my own whilst questioning a befuddled witness. Most of the time I fill in the blanks logically. Sometimes common sense can lead anybody astray. This world sure *looks* flat, and if there was nobody to tell you different you could swear the sun went around the world once a day. But all you really know for certain is that you spied some folks headed your way from that burning schoolhouse and then you were flat on your back next door feeling sort of drained."

Major Sullivan suggested, "Sometimes you forget things as the shock wears off."

Longarm put his notebook away under his frock coat as he shrugged and said, "I reckon. Let's go have a talk with the gent pulling Officer of the Day the night all this took place."

There came an awkward silence. Then Major Sullivan said, "I can let you interview Sergeant Folsum from the Post Engineers or Corporal Arnold from the Quartermasters. They were pulling Sergeant and Corporal of the Guard that evening."

Longarm raised an eyebrow. "Neither one of those names seem to be signed to that final official report on file. Where's the shavetail who took everything down as the Officer of the Day?"

Major Sullivan sighed and said, "That would be Second Lieutenant Fitzroy, W. R. I'm afraid he's not on the post at the moment."

Longarm asked, "How come? Do you usually furlough the OD on duty during a spell of arson, murder, and safe-cracking?"

The provost marshal awkwardly replied, "I understand Fitzroy was just tranferred to the 10th Cav along the border because Victorio is out with his Bronco Apache again."

Longarm counted to three under his breath and quietly said, "We're going to have us a heart-to-heart talk with your commanding officer right now, or I'm headed into town to catch the next train out!"

Sullivan started to argue. Then he nodded and turned for the door. As Longarm moved to follow, Nurse Ericsson fell in beside him to softly murmur, "I think they're covering something up too. Meet me out back after sunset. I'll be off duty then, and I have something to show you."

Chapter 9

A regiment was commanded by a bird colonel or at least a *brevet* CO with that temporary rank in the peacetime army. President Hayes believed in sound money and a balanced budget. Since Fort Douglas was a corps headquarters, the biggest frog in the puddle had to outrank the brevet bird colonel commanding its Mormon-fighting cavalry regiment. So the corps commander at Post Headquarters was Brevet Brigadier L. J. Mather, West Point '59, the class the stars had fallen upon, along with a good many government-issue grave markers.

So when the general offered Longarm a seat and handed out two decent cigars, Longarm said, "As one old soldier to another, General, what in the fuck are you boys trying to pull on Marshal Billy Vail and me?"

Brevet Brigadier Mather, a friendly smiling gent with frosty eyes that went with his steel-gray hair and Back Bay Boston accent, shot a thoughtful glance at Major Sullivan, who soberly said, "He doesn't seem to be buying our official story, General. He's the one who punched our Lieutenant Colonel Walthers flat that time."

Mather stared coldly at Longarm, who was calmly lighting his cigar, and quietly remarked, "I wouldn't have an ass like Walthers in my command. That's why you won't find him involved in this case in any way, shape, or form, Deputy Long. Now suppose you tell me what you think we're trying to cover up.''

Longarm shook out his match, took a drag on the expensive Havana, and blew expensive smoke out his nostrils before he replied, ''If I knew, it wouldn't be covered worth mention, would it? I can't put my finger on it, General. But in my line of work you hear a heap of tales, and some of them make more sense than others, no offense. To begin with, if I buy the version you seem to be out to peddle, there'd be no good reason for all this bullshit about having to send clean out of the territory for somebody like me.''

Mathis shot another look at Sullivan, who insisted, ''I told him we had our own good reasons for leaving the local Mormons out of it.''

Longarm said, ''I was there. I heard you, Major. That never gave me call to buy the notion. It makes no sense. The civilians who administer and police this neck of the woods have no dog in any fight you've been able to sell me.''

''The murdered girl was a Mormon,'' snapped the frosty CO behind the imposing desk.

To which Longarm replied, ''Temple Lot Mormon from back East, who'd have meant no more to the bigwigs of the nearby Salt Lake Temple than any other Gentile killed by government dependents or employees on this U.S. Army post. After that, whether they felt sorry for Miss Petula or not, you'd be asking paid-up Utah lawmen who know this territory and its population better than any of us to help catch seven wanted criminals in no way affiliated with the Church of Jesus Christ of Latter-Day Saints. Add it up. What difference would it have made if you'd raised a public outcry the morning after, except to make it a tad tougher for them to have gotten away? None of them are Mormons, as far as I've heard. So we're talking about a gal of striking looks riding with a half-dozen total strangers and eighteen hundred in cash. They should have been caught by this time if you'd called on the local lawmen for help and they're still in Utah Territory. So how come none of the Mormon lawmen I've talked to friendly, so far, were ever told to watch for such a bunch at the railroad stations in either Ogden or Salt Lake City?''

Mathis coldly replied, ''Suppose you tell us, seeing you're so smart.''

Longarm got to his feet, saying, ''I'm only as smart as the powers that be allow, General. I'd only be guessing if I suggested you don't want any of that bunch picked up by Mormon lawmen lest they tell said Mormon lawmen something you don't want them to hear. Seeing you don't want this child to hear it either, we'll just say no more about it and I'll wire Billy Vail from town that I'm headed back to Colorado.''

Mather said, ''Oh, sit down and listen tight. Once upon a time there was a Mormon War. It wasn't much, as wars go, but a lot of feelings as well as a few people got hurt. A cavalry captain named Worthington got picked off by a Mormon sniper, leading a gallant charge across a salt flat. It was gallant as well as stupid. So they awarded him a medal after he lay too dead to cause any more trouble, and after a time his widow married another officer and was posted out here with him and the son in his teens she'd had by her first marriage, Bobby Worthington of more recent notoriety.''

Longarm thought and started to reach for his notebook, but then he felt safe to say, ''Bobby Worthington, Will Callahan, and Sammy Kraft got accused along with Zenobia Lowell in that letter that Temple Lot Mormon gal sent the IG. But ain't it all likely to come out in the wash as soon as the bunch of them are caught?''

Mather shrugged and said, ''We were planning on holding their trials somewhere else. Anywhere else. That wayword son of an old dead hero may be salvageable. If he was only standing by, we might be able to let him turn state's evidence against the older degenerates who led him astray.''

"Unless he's the leader," Longarm pointed out. "The gal might or might not have been allowing the whole bunch to use her as their play-pretty. That ain't saying *she* was the leader, or even the willing participant, when *somebody* decided it was time to rob that safe, tie that gal in the cellar, and set the schoolhouse on fire. What if you've picked an abducted play-pretty as the leader?"

Mather said, "We'd like to see some of that money they rode off with too. If they're still in the territory, they must be laying low along with the money, or most of it. How much of that war chest would you expect those Mormons to turn over to us if they found it first?"

Longarm shrugged and said, "I'd trust a Saint with a badge at least as far as I'd trust the late Sheriff Brady of Lincoln County. I'd like a look at that safe and a talk with anybody still on the post who'd have had the keys or combination."

That request turned out to be easier to grant. Brevet brigadiers were too important to get up off their asses, of course. But Sullivan led Longarm down the corridor to Post Operations, where another major called Robbins jumped up from his own desk and seemed proud to show the way back to a big Mosler combination safe that looked intact enough to Longarm.

When he said so, Robbins sighed and said, "I'm afraid our Trooper Weems somehow learned the combination. No enlisted man was supposed to know it. I know *I* never gave it to Weems. But as a clerk typist he had plenty of opportunity to watch as authorized personnel worked the three-number combination."

Again, Longarm felt no call to check his own penciled notes as he nodded and said, "Trooper Glover says he first spied that bunch down the other way, as if coming from the direction of a burning schoolhouse. That ain't saying nobody is allowed to slip into an office he's familiar with and open a combination safe a tad earlier that night."

Major Sullivan suddenly said, "I'm beginning to see why

you ask so many nosy questions, Deputy Long. I've been getting a better picture of that confusing night myself as you keep raking over the same coals!''

Longarm said, "They ain't the same coals. They only *look* like the same coals. But each witness I pester is recalling the same events from a different direction. I ain't looking forward to it either, but I reckon we're going to have to question the kith and kin of those three missing schoolboys now.''

They had plenty of time and everybody on the post was within easy walking distance, unfortunately.

Willy Callahan and Sammy Kraft were the elder sons of two married sergeants, both of whom were on duty when Longarm and the major came calling at their family quarters, and that was likely just as well.

Maggie Callahan, a bird-like prim-lipped matron of the Lace Curtain Irish persuasion, invited them in for tea, and only the shaking of her hands betrayed what had to be going through her mind as she quietly but firmly insisted there had to be some mistake. She told them, and Longarm believed her, that her Willy and his younger brother and sister went to Mass every Sunday and that she'd never heard her Willy say one disrespectful word about his schoolmarm. She asked if they didn't think it was possible her boy had been forced to go along by a dreadful bunch of godless Protestants. Longarm told her anything was possible, and asked if her Willy owned a gun.

She swore he'd only owned the single-shot .22 varmint rifle that was still in his closet if they wanted to see it. They declined, and told her they'd get back to her as soon as they knew more about her boy.

Sammy Kraft's Dutch-American mother was fatter and more excitable as she blubbered at them about her poor baby being led down the primrose path by devil-worshipping Papists.

He'd left behind half a box of .32-short rimfire cartridges, but not the whore pistol they went with. His sobbing mother hadn't cracked open the book he'd left behind in its plain brown-paper wrapper. It was a well-thumbed edition of *The Unhappy Valley*. He'd likely held on to his own copy of *Justine*. Longarm told Major Sullivan he was sorry he'd ever questioned that detail, and added, "Like I said, there has to be some place over in the city where you can buy this sort of reading in bulk."

They told Mrs. Kraft they'd let her know as soon as they learned a thing about her boy, and headed over to Officer's Row, where the mother of that dead hero's only son told them she'd been commanded by her new husband not to talk to anyone without him or his civilian lawyer on hand.

Longarm was just as glad. She was one of those otherwise-skinny blue-eyed brunettes with big tits, and he'd never met one yet who wasn't inclined to get hysterical no matter what you asked of them.

By that time they were fixing to line up on the parade for Retreat, and Longarm told the major he'd about talked to everybody he needed to at Fort Douglas. He had no call not to level with a pal of Billy Vail, but he didn't have to tell him everything.

Major Sullivan didn't want to get caught in the open as they lowered the flag. No matter where you were on an army post when that bugle call commenced, you were supposed to stop in your tracks and face toward the flagstaff whether you could see it or not.

So Sullivan got Longarm under cover at the BOQ so the Charge of Quarters could fix him up for the night with one of the modest but private rooms bachelor officers or civilian guests of Longarm's civil-service rank rated.

They looked over the clean spartan cubbyhole with its army cot and field desk with folding chair while, outside, the bugle blew and then, Fort Douglas being a corps headquarters, the band struck up a rousing rendition of *Rally Round the Flag*. It was likely just as well no well-remembered marching songs had been composed for the

71

Mormon War. You could likely hear that band halfway in to the Salt Lake Temple.

After things quieted down again, Major Sullivan allowed he meant to have his own supper at home with his own family. Longarm was just as glad he hadn't been invited to tag along. Aside from pissing any wife off, such unexpected visits tended to drag on over coffee and cigars whether you'd been asked to meet somebody else after hours or not.

Longarm shook and parted friendly with the provost marshal at his office near the guardhouse, and toted his possibles and rifle over to the BOQ for safekeeping in the room assigned to him.

Then he went back to the officer's mess to sup with others lacking a woman of their own on post to serve them home cooking.

That was likely why the officer's mess served shit on a shingle, or chipped beef on toast, as the main entree that evening. The chef had to work harder at noon, when most all the big brass ate there. So he made up for it in the evening by keeping things simple. Longarm hardly ever ate okra, even when it was cooked right. But the fried spuds weren't bad, and army coffee was always strong. So Longarm drank an extra cup, resisted the impulse to leave a lousy tip for the lousy meal he'd already had to pay for, and ambled upslope to the hospital some more. Everything at Fort Douglas was upslope or downslope because they'd built the place on at least a nine-degree grade where no Mormons had been farming. The Latter-Day Saints were fiends for irrigating and cultivating any patch of halfway flat semidesert in what they still liked to call their state of Deseret.

Longarm won bar bets now and again on Deseret. According to the folks who called Utah Territory Deseret, it didn't refer to any real desert. That Angel Moroni had assured them the word meant "honey bee" in some old-time lingo. Longarm never argued with Lakota about the exact meaning of *Wakan* either. It was easier to get along with folks when you let them tell you what they meant, as long as they weren't hurting anybody else.

So he approached the now-dark rear entrance of the post hospital with an open mind, curious but content to let Nurse Ericsson show him what she aimed to show him in her own good time.

He didn't see her where he was expecting to. She'd changed into a darker outfit, and hissed at him from the shadows of a toolshed down a piece from some back steps. As they met, Longarm ticked his hat brim to her and began, "Evening, ma'am. You wanted to show me something?"

The buxom blonde replied, "Not here. My private quarters are just up the slope. Let's go."

She took him by one elbow and led him toward a long one-story red sandstone building with one end of its frame veranda way higher than the other as she said, "Dr. Sloan is a man, trained in wound surgery. But he has the medical degree I lack. So I wasn't able to convince him, or even talk to him about *pseudohymenal labia minora* or an artificial cherry, as the more vulgar prefer to call the condition."

As they mounted the steps, she continued in a lower but surprisingly clinical tone, considering the topic. "Few men have ever seen the rare intact hymen of a virgin who led a very inactive childhood because by the time they've known any woman that well she no longer *had* an intact hymen. The hymen is a tissue-thin membrane that serves no purpose once a girl has matured enough for her natural secretions to keep dust from collecting down there. It's often been torn and withered away long before any man needs to do such honors. But there is this rarer quirk of nature that can be mistaken for virginity. I'm not sure whether you would call it a curse or a blessing. I only know I was born with it. So I feel it's my duty to show you my privates in the name of the law."

Chapter 10

Nurse Ericsson allowed that her friends called her Frida as she sat her bemused guest down on a sofa and told him to make himself at home while she changed into something more comfortable for her anatomy lesson. So when she ducked out of her small parlor, Longarm shucked his hat and coat and, as long as he was standing, his gunbelt, hoping she wouldn't think him forward since she'd only offered to *show* him her old ring-dang-doo.

She didn't say one way or the other when she came back in, carrying coffee and cake on a German silver salver without a stitch on above her thighs. He tried not to grin like a shit-eating dog as she calmly set the refreshments on the rosewood coffee table in front of the sofa.

It wasn't easy. She was still wearing her high-button shoes with white thigh-high stockings, and her ash-blond hair was still pinned up formally as she turned to throw one long leg up to brace an ankle on the backrest of the sofa and settle down to face him, wide open to the world, with her other foot still planted on the floor. "I'll cut the cake and pour the coffee as soon as we get this anatomy lesson out of the way," she said. "Don't stare at my breasts. You can see they're perfectly normal. It's my unusual vagina I wanted you to look at!"

As she settled her naked Junoesque torso back against the padded arm of the sofa at her end, Longarm soberly stared down at the pink gash parting the thick blond thatch between her big shapely thighs and managed to reply, "I'm looking, and I purely admire all I can see from here, Miss Frida. No offense, but your pretty little ring-dang-doo doesn't strike me as all that strange. *Tempting* as all get-out, I'll allow. But I don't see anything to qualify you for Mister Barnum's sideshow."

She moistened two fingers with her mouth and placed them between her thighs to part the *labia majora* or fuzzy lips as she invited him to lean forward for a closer look.

When he did, he could see that the pinker, thinner, and moister inner lips that usually didn't part as wide, but still parted, seemed to stick together down yonder, as if to bar the way in, the way they said that pesky obstruction called a cherry might. Her point about them being rare had been well taken. Peering closer, he saw the way into this gal sure looked closed to the general public. So he said so.

She said, "Put a finger there and see how easily it goes in."

To which he felt obliged to reply, "I'd rather not, ma'am. I suffer from a genital condition of my own. Being a trained nurse, you've no doubt heard of it. It's called an erection, and try as I might, I've no control of the way my old organ-grinder seems to rise to such an occasion as sticking my fingers up a lady's privates."

She used her other hand to show him how she could slip two of her own fingers through what seemed the pink wet barrier as she calmly said, "I'm sorry if this arouses you. I was only trying to show you how that girl who died in that fire could have been more experienced than Dr. Sloan suggests in his official autopsy. Would you like to try penetrating me with that erection you just mentioned, if only in the name of the law, of course?"

Seeing she'd put it that way, Longarm was out of his duds and into her unusual plumbing in no time, and whether she felt it was only an anatomy lesson or not, she kissed wet and wild as he lowered his own naked flesh atop and into hers. So neither tried to mar the magic as they just indulged in some old-fashioned rutting and allowed their healthy muscular bodies to get well acquainted. The big Scandinavian blonde was in prime shape from nigh thirty years of honest work, and could have licked most men in an honest wrestling match had she not liked screwing men better.

Longarm was too polite to ask if she'd wanted to do what they were doing from the first moment they'd met. He knew gals liked to hear such wicked things, and she laughed like hell and called him a rogue when he came in her hard, spread her legs wider, and declared, "Enough of this foreplay! I've been wanting to fuck you all afternoon!"

She said she'd admired his shoulders some before she'd thought she ought to do her duty as a concerned citizen and warn a lawman about an autopsy report that could be read more than one way.

They sat bare-ass, side by side on the sofa, to share coffee and cake. She seemed to want to get back to the detached clinical tone she was more comfortable with. He wasn't about to ask how a gal with such a warm nature had come by such a cool protective veil. He was afraid she might tell him. You could love 'em and leave 'em and no harm done when you only got into a lady's old ring-dang-doo. But they never forgave you when you rode on and left them behind after they'd let you get inside their hopes and hurts. He could tell old Frida had gotten hurt after some hoping. So he was content to go along with her game of just not hoping or asking for more than the moment. She made swell coffee too.

As they sipped some, with her hand in his lap to gently fondle his limp virility with more skill than most gals managed without medical training, Frida asked Longarm what he thought the army was out to cover up. He said he wasn't sure, and asked her why she thought anybody was out to cover anything.

She said, "I told you how I tried to tell Dr. Sloan he didn't know what he was talking about when he told me to type up that autopsy report. I thought at first he was just being stuffy and know-it-all. But when I mentioned *pseudohymenal labia minora*, a textbook medical condition, and volunteered I had it myself, he got as hysterical as you saw him this afternoon. It's as if he's under orders to record the death of that Mormon girl one way and one way alone."

Longarm nodded thoughtfully and said, "I'd be obliged if you'd either let go or move your hand faster, Miss Frida. I did notice the doc was acting upset. In front of that military lawman too. But the major and my own boss, Marshal Vail, go back to hunting Comancheros together, and I've seldom seen an honest officer go bad so late in the game."

She began to stroke faster as she asked, "What if your own superiors were fooled and he only seemed honest because there was nothing at the time to lie about? What's a Comanchero anyhow? I keep hearing about them but I've never had any dealings with Comanche Indians."

Longarm shook his head and moved his hips in time with her pecker-pulling as he replied, "It's never been that easy to fool Billy Vail, and he told me Major Sullivan's all right. A Comanchero ain't no Indian. He's a Tex-Mex dealer in contraband, or he was. The Comanche ain't had a heap of stolen livestock to swap for firewater and trade goods since they lost the Buffalo War. I'd hate to waste what I have to give you in your pretty little hand, Miss Frida. Why don't we see if you look as much like a virgin dog-style?"

She laughed, let go, and turned to kneel on the leather cushions with her bare breasts propped over the far arm of the sofa as she thrust her broad but shapely bare ass up at him, demurely insisting, "I still say they're trying to cover up something naughty."

Longarm rose to plant one foot on the floor and one knee on the sofa behind her as he took a cheek in either hand to spread them wider for a good peer down at her slit. He'd just been in there with a full erection, and it still looked as if entry was barred by a pink partition of moist chastity. He was able to watch closer as he moved the head of his own trembling desire into position and thrust slowly to see it sort of walking through a wall like a horny haunt. From that angle, with the table lamp shedding more light on the subject, he could see the inner lips that were usually parted at such times were thicker than those of more natural gals. But even though they tended to stay pursed tightly together, left to their druthers, they parted as wide as anything pushing between them needed them to part. She moaned in pleasure as he drove in all the way, and he had to allow that that ring of wet tightness sliding the length of his reinspired shaft felt mighty fine!

He began to thrust with long slow strokes as he observed, "You've convinced me neither Zenobia Lowell, the schoolmarm, nor Petula Dorman, her pupil, can be eliminated as a sex fiend. That's what we call what I'm doing, the process of eliminating."

She arched her spine to take it deeper as she replied, "Really? I thought you were fucking me. Are you suggesting the younger girl made up those things she wrote the IG about her older teacher, or rival? I told you Dr. Sloan was wrong about the body we examined having to be a virgin. I never said I thought it was Zenobia Lowell. I don't see how it could have been. Personnel had the schoolmarm they were paying as an experienced employee of thirty-two. The sutler said his daughter, Petula, had just turned sixteen. Could you move a little faster, dear?"

He could and did, saying, "Zenobia Lowell seemed to be built sort of boyish in that one photograph, and some gals mature earlier than others. Your turn."

Frida moaned, "Faster! Harder! I don't see why the army would want to cover up for either woman, but I still say the younger one died in that fire and the other rode off with the gang and ooooh, I'm coming!"

It was taking more time for the man stuck with most of the work. So Longarm was talking mostly to himself as he mused aloud, "Miss Zenobia works better as the leader in any case. We did recover one of those dirty books the younger gal reported to the IG, and if those kids had been getting them and reading them without any help from an older depraved gal, they'd have had no call to kill anybody. They would have found some other place for their orgies and neither their schoolmarm nor the inspector general would have had to be pestered."

She didn't answer, in words, as she went limp to sag swayback, with him still grinding away with a hand gripping each widely spaced hip bone while she bit down in a friendly way with her innards.

Then he didn't feel like talking either, and she seemed to take it as a warm compliment when he whipped it out to turn her over and spread her thighs far and wide again and finish "so sweetly!" as she called it.

She coyly said, "I felt that!" when he came in her and had the good manners to keep most of his weight on his elbows.

He kissed her again and murmured, "I did too. It ain't fair. Us men have a hell of a time pretending we like one of you gals when we don't."

She stiffened under him and asked just what that was supposed to mean.

He kissed her some more and said soothingly, "I ain't talking about us. I'm talking about wicked gals in general. I've often suspected a total man-hating gal makes the most convincing whore or con artist. Just before I came out this way I helped them arrest a pretty little thing who'd married up with an ugly old mining man for his money. He sure had nothing *else* to offer any gals. There was no way for him to tell how much she despised him, before he caught her in the act with somebody she liked better. You gals can hate a man's guts and still give him a swell screwing. Us poor souls just ain't built that way. If I didn't like you a heap, it wouldn't still be so hard inside of you, see?"

She bit down with her love muscles and wrapped her legs

around him more comfortably, for her. He'd have enjoyed it more had she been out of her shoes and socks. But just as he was about to say so, and mention a move to the bedroom, Frida said, "All right. Just one more. But then you have to go, dear. I share this parlor with another nurse, and while she's on night duty and we take turns sleeping, we do come over from the hospital near the end of each shift to wake each other up. I don't know what she'd say if she came over in the cold gray dawn and found us in bed together, so . . ."

He cut in. "Say no more. Let me get my breath back and we'll part friendly. I have a bunk of my own over to the BOQ and it's early yet."

So they wound up with her on top because she was lighter and there was no comfortable way to lie side by side and smoke aboard a leather sofa, as nice as it was for fornication.

He puffed on her nipples instead, once she was in his lap and vice versa. Neither one tasted anything like a three-for-a-nickel cheroot, but he didn't mind and he said so.

She tittered and leaned closer, kissing the part in his hair before she said, "Be serious. I really want to know. What do you think those officers are keeping from the rest of us? You don't buy the official version of what happened that dreadful night, do you?"

He replied with one nipple in the corner of his mouth, "I do and I don't. The tale of a wicked schoolmarm leading some pupils astray and then the whole bunch killing a tattletale and riding off with the garrison war chest holds together, down to every detail."

She began to slowly post in the saddle with her big tits in his face as she murmured, "Oooh, nice! You have a lovely body and I wish I had these quarters all to myself. Where do you feel the story falls apart, Custis?"

He said, "The *story* don't. Those charges made to the IG were sort of serious. There's no telling what Petula Dorman might have charged in a letter the IG never got. The schoolmarm so charged is missing. The pupils she was said to be leading astray are missing. The garrison war chest is missing, and the gal who told tales out of school is dead. It ain't what the accused are accused of that bothers me. It's what the army expects anybody else to *do* about them that bothers me. You're so right about Major Sullivan acting as if he was sorry to see me when I got here, even though it was his grand notion to send away for me, or at least somebody like me.

"They told me they didn't send their regular military police out after one wicked schoolmarm and a gang of mean kids because they figured it would take somebody who knew the Utah Territory to track them across all those irrigation ditches and salt flats. But then they told me they didn't want any local Mormon lawmen tracking them lest the Mormon newspapers say . . . what? What's so damned sensitive about the case from a Mormon point of view? The only Mormon at all involved was a member of what the Salt Lake Temple considers a misguided sect. After that, she was a *victim,* not a victimizer. All the fugitives the provost marshal says he wants caught are outsiders as far as any resident of Utah Territory, Mormon or Gentile, has any call to say. The local newspapers carry news about Frank and Jesse or Billy the Kid without blaming their dastardly deeds on the U.S. Army or Federal Government. So why me and not the dozens of other lawmen who know this country and its denizens on both sides of the law so much better?"

She began to move up and down faster as she casually suggested the provost marshal might not want Mormon lawmen talking to those deserters and schoolboys about something else they might have done.

Longarm started to object, thought, grinned up at her, and declared, "I want to get on top again. For you've just said something smart as hell and I aim to reward you in the best way I know how."

81

Chapter 11

Time had a way of passing fast when you were having fun. So it was after midnight by the time Longarm got back to the BOQ walking a little stiff, and lit a table lamp to make some notes before he got undressed again.

It was just as well he was still wearing his shirt and vest when he heard sneaky tapping at the window and felt the hairs rising on the back of his neck when he glanced up to see a pale ghostly face hanging outside in the darkness.

Then he recognized the matronly but still handsome features of that dead hero's widow and present captain's wife, the mother of young Bobby Worthington.

He wasn't wearing a hat to tip, and his gunbelt was hung up for the night as well. So he just stood up and went over to open the window and say, "Evening, ma'am. I thought you said you didn't want to talk with us about your boy and, no offense, ain't it a mite late if you've gone and changed your mind?"

She said, "Help me over the sill. It's getting cold out here!"

He could feel the no-longer-balmy breezes blowing up her skirts as she forked a leg sheathed in black silk and exposed to the knee over the low sill. Her pleated bodice and ruffled skirts were black poplin. Her hair made up for her sober outfit by shining auburn in the lamplight as he helped her fork her way inside and tried not to imagine what she had on under the skirts as she slid her crotch over the sill.

Once he had her standing in a more dignified positon on his side of the sill, she asked him to shut the window and draw the blind so they could be assured of complete privacy.

He did as she asked. He knew that since she was an army wife, had been more than once, she had to know that the enlisted Charge of Quarters was within earshot at the far end of the corridor outside, whether any officers were bedded down for the night to either side or not.

He kept his own voice low as he repeated what he'd said about her telling him and Major Sullivan her husband had forbidden her to talk to them alone.

She softly replied, "I lied. I didn't want to say anything more in front of that treacherous provost marshal. He put words in my mouth in the official report he filed about my Bobby and those other boys. You have to understand that my Bobby is a *good* boy. He might be just a bit wild. It's something he's going through, and my present husband doesn't feel it's his place to strike another man's grown son."

Longarm quietly suggested, "I wasn't planning on spanking any of those boys, ma'am. How come you're fooling with my buttons that way? If you're trying to help me out of this vest, you're aimed too low."

She snatched her hand from the front of his pants with a flustered gasp and said, "Oh, forgive me. It's just a silly habit I've fallen into when arguing with my husband about Bobby. My child does not need to be . . . examined. Being interested in . . . adult subjects is simply part of growing up to be a real man. You understand that, don't you? I can see you're a real man. My first husband, Bobby's father, was a real man. Unlike an administrative officer I know, he died at the head of his troop, leading the charge."

Longarm said, "They told me. The late Petula Dorman never accused your first husband of anything, ma'am. She only accused your son of handing in book reports on books not to be found in your post library. If it's any comfort to you, I'm keeping an open mind as to who did what with what to whom until we round up the whole bunch and see if somebody wants to tell us. Speaking from experience, gang members who feel they ain't as guilty tend to turn state's evidence against the ringleaders."

She put her fingertips to his fly again without looking down between them as she protested, "Bobby's not a member of any *gang*! He was only trying to improve his mind. He'd have never hurt that sutler's daughter, or agreed to go along with such a thing. He *likes* girls. He's a very warm-natured youth!"

Longarm gently but firmly took her by the wrist to move her hand away, saying, "That seems to run in his family, no offense. To save us both a dumb wrassle, I'd best tell you up front that there is just no way on earth a lawman who may have to testify against a suspect in a capital-punishment case is about to play slap and tickle with the boy's own mother!"

She blushed beet red, turned away, and sat down on his army cot to cover her face with both hands and blubber.

Longarm remained on his feet as he told her not unkindly, "If I was that weak-natured in the tempting here and now, I'd still have to ride after the bunch of them in the cold gray dawn. I don't suppose you have the least notion where your boy might be tonight?"

She didn't answer.

He nodded soberly and said, "All right. Here's the best deal I can offer. If you're boy's had second thoughts and doubled back to ask his momma for help, you're going about it all wrong. I'd be lying and you'd know I was lying if I said I didn't want to lay you. I'm a man and you must have at least one mirror over to your own quarters. But that could backfire on you and your boy as well. Neither the arresting officer nor a character witness cut much ice in court when it can be shown they've been playing slap and tickle with anybody else on either side. I take it you want me to see if they'll let your boy off in exchange for his testifying against somebody worse?"

She nodded mutely without uncovering her face.

He said, "I don't like to break my word at times like this, for the same reasons I don't want to drop my drawers. I'd have to know how deep your boy might be mired in such a sticky mess. A boy in his teens running away from home is a matter for his own folks to settle. Neither your Bobby nor the Callahan or Kraft boy can be charged with desertion. Has he told you or his stepfather whose notion it was to lay hands on that Temple Lot Mormon gal, or the garrison war chest?"

She dropped her hands to her lap and stared up at him with tears running down her cheeks as she replied, "My husband knows nothing of what's going on. He says he doesn't *want* to know. He says such a scandal isn't going to do a thing for the career of a man who's already overage in grade and that he'd leave me if I didn't do exactly as the general and that awful provost marshal say!"

Longarm smiled thinly and said, "Some men would know better than to argue with a she-bear defending her cub. Let's get back to what Bobby told you. Who might he have named as the baddest apple in the barrel, and whilst we're at it, where's he at?"

She said, "He told me you'd ask both those questions. He warned me not to tell you anything before you promised he wouldn't have to go to jail once he told you what you wanted to know."

Longarm said, "We're talking in circles, ma'am. I'll tell you what I'm willing to give my word on. I'll meet your boy private, out on the open range, and I'll hear what he has to say. If I like what I hear, we can ride back here together on such terms as we've both agreed to. If we can't make a deal, I'll treat the parley as if we'd met under a flag of truce and he can ride out of sight with a full hour's lead before I go after him.''

She hesitated, then asked, "How can we be sure you won't just arrest him on sight? The general is very cross with all of them.''

Longarm replied in a no-nonsense tone, "How do you know I wouldn't have screwed you bowlegged and double-crossed you anyhow? I have a certain advantage over some officers and gentlemen. I don't claim to be no gentleman. But I'll bet you a month's pay you can't find a human being, in jail or out, who can say I gave them my word and busted it!''

She sighed, rose to her feet, and held out a hand as she told him to call on her at her own quarters around ten in the morning.

He didn't know what he was supposed to do with her fool hand, so he just shook it as he protested, "That's too late in the day, ma'am. Come morning, earlier, I mean to borrow me a mount and ride over to Salt Lake City in search of shady bookshops and other such notions.''

She sounded as if she meant it when she insisted, "You'll have to do things my way, with or without your pants on. I have to see whether Bobby is agreeable to your suggestion. He's not on post. I can tell you that much. So I have to drive into town and back myself before I'll be able to tell you another thing.''

Longarm started to argue, shrugged, and trimmed the lamp so they could sneak her out the window the same way she got in. She said not to come knocking, lest they disturb her husband with matters he didn't want to discuss. Then she surprised him with a far from matronly kiss on the lips and hissed, "Be there!'' before she draped her crotch back over the windowsill and slipped away in the moonlight.

As soon as she was gone, Longarm pulled the blind down again and lit a match long enough to check some names in his notebook. Then he ducked out and moved down the corridor to where the enlisted CQ was reading a magazine behind the key desk. The army kept closer tabs on single men's private quarters than most hotels. A bachelor officer who wanted to sneak a gal in had to drag her crotch over the windowsill. Longarm had to wonder how often Bobby Worthington's dear old mother had entered or left a BOQ that way before.

She wasn't using the name of her first husband now. So Longarm got out a cheroot for the corporal stuck for the night with CQ, and lit him up before he casually asked, "You wouldn't know who's pulling HQ, CQ, or OD at this hour, would you, pard?"

The man, who was only in charge of those particular quarters for the night, replied without hesitation, "Sure I would. Officer of the Day would be Lieutenant Hershey. Captain Bradford is holding down the general's desk for him tonight."

Longarm nodded and said, "Somebody told me Captain Bradford might have the day off come morning. Figured he had to be pulling night duty. You say the OD would be named Hershey? He'd be over to the guardhouse betwixt rounds, right?"

The CQ shrugged and allowed he guessed so. Longarm went back to his room, locked the door, hauled on his six-gun, hat, and coat, and rolled over the same windowsill in the dark to leg his way over to the guardhouse. He didn't have to guess who might be where now. As an army vet who'd scouted some since, Longarm knew that once they'd blown Retreat and let most of the outfit off for the night, all the desks that were at all important to the running of a corps headquarters by day had to be manned by lesser lights through the night in the event of any unexpected emergency. So Bobby Worthington's stepfather was at post headquarters for the night, and where did that leave Bobby and his dear old sneaky mom?

The Officer of the Day, stuck with acting as a sort of chief of police after duty hours, left most of the running around in the dark to the Corporal of the Guard. So Longarm found Lieutenant Hershey in the guardhouse, lounging by the unlit stove in a rocking chair and watching the Sergeant of the Guard clean a Springfield .45-70 on the front counter.

Longarm introduced himself and got right to the point. He told the officer who was in position to smooth his path, "I just got a tip and I have to ride into town on the sneak right now. I don't want to bother your remount and I really don't want anyone to know I'm riding off post. But you're the OD and you have the right to know everything that's going on."

It worked. The younger officer rose with a smile, pleased by the courtesy and just as glad to have something to do. He led Longarm out front to point out the bay gelding Longarm had noticed coming in. The cavalry mount was tethered with a nose bag, but saddled and bridled to go, as the junior officer unbuckled the nose bag and handed Longarm the reins, saying, "I call him Shoshone and he must be as bored as I am. So I can walk my rounds if I have to, and I doubt like hell I'll have to. How long did you say you'd be off post with him?"

Longarm truthfully replied, "I don't know. Like I said, I just got a tip I want to follow up on. I'm here at the request of your provost marshal to look into that arson, murder, and robbery you had out here and—"

"Major Sullivan told us about you, Longarm," the young officer said, adding with a boyish grin, "You didn't think I'd lend my favorite mount to a Mormon elder, did you?"

Longarm said, "Aw, they've been making me wear this sissy suit on duty since President Hayes and his Lemonade Lucy took over back East. I'm much obliged, and I'll try to get Shoshone back to you soon as well as safe and sound, hear?"

As he mounted up, Hershey asked, "Who tipped you off about what in town? You're not after those three deserters, are you?"

Longarm said, "I'd tell you if I knew where they were

to be found. I understand you're the one with the jurisdiction, Lieutenant. I hope to meet a possible witness. I told the one who set it up I wouldn't say nothing as long as all concerned behaved themselves.''

The officer, who didn't look old enough to have been in the war, said, ''Say no more. I understand the rules of Parley. I won't have to write this conversation up in my morning report unless somebody shoots you riding on or off the post. So good hunting and try not to lose my horse!''

Longarm laughed and rode, not toward the gate, as one might expect, but due south toward nothing much but silvery sage in the moonlight as Shoshone carried him at a walk between the last two sandstone outbuildings at that end of the unfenced fort.

He'd been braced for a challenge and at least a few words with an interior guard. But the kid walking that post in a military manner was walking it somewhere else, if he wasn't jacking off. So once Longarm found himself out in the clear, he reined the bay west toward town and heeled him into a brisk lope. He knew anybody driving on the gravel wagon trace to town would hear hoofbeats *following* them. So he rode in line but well off to the side of the regular route, hoping to get well ahead of Bobby Worthington's sneaky little momma before he cut over to see where she might be headed as he let her drive past.

Chapter 12

The lady had dragged her crotch over that sill about twenty minutes ahead of his, and it wouldn't have taken her as long to order a carriage hitched up to drive into town. It might have taken her longer if she'd done her own hitching on the sneak lest her new husband find out about it later. Either way, he doubted she'd be driving as fast as a man out to head her off could ride a good cavalry mount over range it knew, but if she was, a man would be out of luck.

The City of the Saints had been built up over a mile from the Salt Lake Temple grounds by then, and there were truck and dairy farms as far upslope as Mormon ingenuity could manage. Old Jim Bridger had offered to bet a dollar for every ear of corn they'd ever raise in the high and dry Great Basin, and it had been a good thing for him Brother Brigham hadn't held with gambling. Inventions like the Mormon plow and plain hard work had diked, terraced, and irrigated most everywhere east of the Great Salt Lake where you could get water to flow halfway slow. So Longarm was skirting fences and jumping ditches less than a mile from the military post, and as he loped in sight of the outskirts of town, he came to a north-south avenue planed flat and wide for future town lots by those same Mormon plows— funny-looking inventions consisting of an axle and two cart wheels at one end of a long pole, and a sort of barn door broadside to the other, with the draft team between able to shove dirt ahead like a snowplow if they put their backs into it, as oxen would when the teamster knew his job.

Longarm reined to a quieter walk, and moved north to where the westbound road from Fort Douglas crossed the avenue near the current city limits. The crossing stood stark in the moonlight. Longarm walked his willing bay over to where a real-estate sign faced the crossing in front of a grove of scrub oak. He dismounted to stand behind the sign with old Shoshone. He let the pony graze the bluestem he was standing in for now, but kept the reins short on his left hand as he peered to the east, up the road from Fort Douglas.

The waning, but still fat, moon was high, and the mountains rising just beyond the fort against a darker starry sky looked closer than they really were, although they weren't nearly as far from town as the Front Range loomed west of Denver. He could make out a few pinpoints of lamplight from the direction of the fort. He was afraid he'd gotten there too late. He'd noticed that that gal seemed to *move* once her mind got set on something. He was tempted to scout about for her some. He didn't. There were potential hideouts in every direction, and when folks hid out, it was *supposed* to be tough to spot where they'd gone.

Then he could hear the distant clop of trotting hooves and the jingle of carriage harness. Shoshone heard it as well, and raised his muzzle from the bluestem as if to nicker a greeting to a fellow horse. But Longarm gently clamped his other palm to the bay's nostrils and told Shoshone to just hush. So the well-trained cavalry mount did. It knew as well as its experienced rider that a horse couldn't breathe enough to carry on a loud conversation with a man's hand cupped over its muzzle.

There was no law of man or nature saying nobody else could drive into town from Fort Douglas after midnight. But as the one-horse sulky reached the crossroads, Longarm could see the driver and sole occupant was a trim-waisted woman wearing a duster and veiled hat.

She turned north at the crossing without hesitation, and Longarm remounted to follow. He couldn't help wondering whether she was just in a hurry, or whether somebody had told her you could walk your mount fairly quietly on dirt or grass, but couldn't sneak after anyone at a trot. He walked Shoshone along the side of the newly graded road at first to let her put some distance between them, then heeled his own mount into a trot through roadside weeds and sagebrush off the moonlit avenue, where he could still make her and her sulky out as a moving black blur.

There were houses lined up on fifty-foot lots to the east of the new avenue now. They all looked alike, and none showed one peep of light, which seemed reasonable for after midnight, or anything like a lawn or garden between them and the road, which didn't. He swung across what would have been somebody's front lawn, if it hadn't been covered with sage and building debris, to have a better look. As he'd suspected, he was following Bobby Worthington's momma along one edge of a housing tract they were still trying to sell off. That accounted for the real-estate sign he and Shoshone had been hunkered behind by the crossroads.

Mormons were like that. The Prophet Joseph Smith had been a Calvinist Protestant before he'd met up with the Angel Moroni in that York State apple orchard, and it seemed as if nobody raised along Calvinist lines had ever been able to just sit still and pray. Salt Lake City and the whole Mormon Delta running north and south of it along the aprons of the Wasatch Range were built up far more than the current population of Utah Territory called for. Some ambitious Saint was always digging another irrigation ditch, grading another road, or building something in that distinctive regional style they seemed to be inventing as they went along, shooting for size and solid construction without trying for any of the classical styles most Victorian architects used.

They sure liked domes and mansard roofs taller than some built back East.

The one-family homes some speculator had run up out this way were two-story cubes with peaked roofs and dormers facing all four ways. He didn't have time to try any doors as he rode past. He knew kids, or passing tramps, could always manage to find a way in. Kids riding back and forth from Fort Douglas in the recent past would have watched this whole tract rise out of the sage, and know all these houses were still standing empty on the outskirts of town.

So Longarm wasn't surprised when that dark blur he was trailing at rifle range swung off the road and came to a stop in the moonlight. He swung Shoshone behind the next empty shell he came to and dismounted, saying, "No offense, but I can walk quieter than you, pard," as he tethered the reins to the latch of the cellar doors so the bay could get to browse the fresh weeds sprouted along the sandstone foundation.

Then he moved around to the back to circle in on foot with his six-gun in hand. The woman had said her boy wanted to give up. But he hadn't done so yet, and somebody in that bunch had to be capable of cold-blooded murder.

He was a little more than halfway between his borrowed mount and the house he'd seen the sulky turn in to when he heard a heartfelt scream. Followed by a single pistol shot.

He knew he was damned if he did and damned if he didn't. But he was closer to the screaming woman than that cavalry mount. So he ran on past the oddly spooky houses looming quieter than quiet in the moonlight, as if haunted by folks who'd yet to move in.

Then he heard hoofbeats and swore in vain as he tore out to the road in time to see another blur, a smaller one, lighting off to the north at full gallop.

Having to make another quick choice, Longarm moved in on the sulky he could make out a couple of yards ahead. Any number of folks could bleed to death while a damned fool ran clean back to his own mount and rode after that other rider, who he might not catch anyway.

Aware there was usually more than one round in your average pistol, Longarm mixed caution with speed in approaching the house the sulky and its pony stood in front of. The front door was closed. He swung to the west to see a side casement window gaping wide. Remembering how that matronly gal could slither her crotch over a windowsill, Longarm eased close, took a deep breath, and risked a peep inside through yet another window.

Moonlight lancing in the front windows at a steep angle drew long rectangles of light across a bare wood floor, save for one place where he could make out a woman's high-button shoe at one corner of such a patch, reminding him of the leftover paw of a mouse an old cat had left in a corner of a bunkhouse one time.

He tapped on the glass with his gun barrel, braced to move like a gob of spit on a hot stove. But nothing happened. That shoe never even twitched at the sound.

He muttered, "Shit, I wasn't expecting to live forever anyhow," as he moved to the open window and rolled over the sill fast, to roll some more across the bare floor planks and rise to one knee in the dark near a far wall, snapping, "I see you! Get them hands up!"

There was no reply to his bluff. He swallowed hard and got all the way to his feet to ease forward. As his eyes adjusted to the darkness ahead, he could make out two darker forms on the floor of the empty front room. One was still attached to that moonlit foot. He moved over to her first, and dropped to his knee again to feel her throat with his free hand. Her flesh still felt soft and warm. There was no pulse. The smell of piss rose mixed with perfume from the folds of her driving outfit.

He moved over to the other form, hunkered down, and quietly said, "I'm afraid your mother is dead if you'd be Bobby Worthington."

The youth sort of smiling up at him from the floor didn't

answer. He smelled pissy too, and when Longarm felt for a pulse the flesh was cold to the touch. Longarm took the body by one wrist and moved the arm, or tried to, before he decided, "You're Bobby Worthington. You've been dead at least six hours. They killed you just after sundown, and waited here until your poor momma came back to talk to you some more. She saw you lying here, and got off that one scream before they got her too."

He rose back to his full considerable height and reached for a smoke to kill the nasty taste in his mouth as he continued, really talking to himself instead of either victim as he tried to picture how they'd wound up there at his feet. "You should have known they wouldn't want you trying to deal yourself out, Bobby. They'd already killed that gal for telling tales out of school, whether she'd gone along with the fun at first or not."

He lit his cheroot, broke the match stem to make sure it was out, and tossed it in the nearby fireplace as he headed back to that window, murmuring, "That's the trouble with getting frisky in large herds. One man and one woman can try most anything they've ever heard of, and go on from there or just drop it if they decide it's too rich for their blood. But once you get wild orgies going, somebody is almost sure to want to get too wild, or get sore when he or she gets refused. Hell hath no fury like a woman scorned, or a volunteer cocksucker who's been told not to be silly."

He climbed back outside and holstered his .44-40 as he jogged back to where he'd tethered his own mount. It gave him time to sort his thoughts some. He warned himself not to draw in too many details as he sketched the most recent killings in his own mind. It was tempting to think the virginity or lack of virginity on the part of that first dead female meant all that much. But in point of fact, a schoolgirl might have reported a schoolmarm who'd disgusted her whether she'd been a virgin or not. And they'd have killed her for telling on them whether she'd been taking part in some of the earlier slap and tickle or not. They'd just proven that point. Bobby Worthington had for certain gone along with the game, to whatever point he'd balked at.

So the question before the house now was *what* he'd balked at. A kid who'd run off with a gang of murderous horse thieves and a garrison war chest would need something worse to shock him to his senses. So they'd been planning something worse, other than killing him and his mother tonight.

He reached Shoshone, untethered him, and mounted up to ride back to the murder scene as he told the bay, "We don't want to move any bodies before they've been photographed in broad daylight. But that other pony can't just stand there until we can get out to the fort and back with an MP detail. So we'd best trail him with us, hear?"

He rode back to the other house and dismounted again to soothe the dead woman's hackney pony and unhitch it from the sulky shafts as he told it what had happened and where they were going. He knew the critter didn't understand a word he was saying, but horses responded to a reassuring tone, and the steppe nomads of the Old World who'd first tamed wild horses doubtless had told them the latest tribal gossip as they'd hitched or unhitched them. Longarm had heard Indians gabbing with their ponies the same way.

So it felt natural to say, "I doubt anybody in the gang will still be holed up in any of these empty tract houses. But they may have left some useful sign, and a corporal's squad fanned out to scout for it is likely to uncover more faster than one poor cuss on his own."

Neither critter had any answer to offer, but it was still something to study on as he led the carriage pony over to Shoshone by its longer reins. He got a grip on all four lengths of leather and swung himself up to head back to Fort Douglas, even as he scowled at the picture of those soldiers blue scouting for sign with him.

Moving back out to the road he muttered, "Some of them may be old Indian fighters. Some may be country boys who've at least hunted game. But an unknown quantity are sure to be city boys who couldn't track an elephant across a fresh-plowed forty. I wish I could ask some Utah lawmen for help with this chore!"

He thought about that some more until they'd almost reached that crossroads. His orders from his own boss, Marshal Billy Vail, had been to offer the army a hand with some fugitives. No more, no less. Billy hadn't said anything about fighting other civilian lawmen over jurisdiction. Whether the army wanted things that way or not, Mormon lawmen, and no doubt the Salt Lake Temple, knew as much as Longarm did about those three gunslicks he'd met up with already, and they were surely fixing to be sore as hell when, not if, they found out he'd found two dead bodies off the post and inside the Salt Lake City limits without having had the common courtesy to mention the matter to them.

So when they got to the crossroads, Longarm swung Shoshone and led the carriage pony west, toward the Salt Lake Temple, as he got out the last smoke he figured to enjoy for a spell and lit up, explaining to the horses and anybody else who might be listening, "Got no choice in the matter. Jurisdiction is jurisdiction no matter what the major says, and Utah riders have to be better at scouting for sign out here in Utah Territory. So we'll cut them in and deal with all the damned cards faceup, and farther along, like the old song goes, we might just see who's trying to deal from the *bottom* of the deck around here!"

Chapter 13

You could say "Salt Lake Temple" to mean the large building looking like a cathedral that they'd started before the war next to the bread-loaf-shaped Mormon Tabernacle, and hadn't finished yet, or you could mean the big council of elders who ran the church and most everything else for many a mile. Neither would be receiving visitors after midnight. So he reined in out front of Salt Lake City Police Headquarters, closer to the railroad depot.

Despite all that travel writers had written, good or bad, the Mormon lawmen who policed the growing city eleven miles east of the Great Salt Lake looked, talked, and acted much the same as any other copper badges Longarm had worked with in the past. Since he'd worked with them in the past, they didn't worry him as much as they seemed to worry Irish-American provost marshals who might not have felt too comfortable sharing military secrets with Southern Baptists when you studied on it.

The Mormon watch commander had heard of Longarm more than once. You could hardly shoot it out with the late Cotton Younger in a Salt Lake City courthouse and not be remembered. They'd been wired about the gunplay the other night up in Ogden, and the watch commander was a tad put out that Longarm hadn't come calling sooner.

Longarm told them flat out there was a jurisdictional problem, and the watch commander sent a runner to fetch the chief of police. They had the two horses from Fort Douglas stabled out back with fodder and water by the time the chief of police showed up, looking more like a bearded undertaker, but talking like a lawman as he wiped sleep-gum from his eyes. So Longarm repeated much of what he'd already told the watch commander and desk sergeant, choosing his words carefully lest he talk too much or flat out lie.

The three Mormon lawmen agreed they sure as shooting had call to cover a double murder committed inside the city limits no matter where the victims had come from or who the head of their house might work for.

Longarm said, "I'd like both bodies examined by somebody less apt to sulk out of the room when you ask simple questions. The virginity of the female victim ain't an issue this time. But I'd still like to have her looked at by a sawbones who'd be more likely to be able to tell."

The chief of police turned to the other Mormons to say, "He's talking about that Gentile schoolgirl who was burned alive out at Fort Douglas last week."

Longarm smiled sheepishly and said, "I should have expected you'd have heard in town. But I was told that the killing was delicate because in point of fact Miss Petula Dorman was not a Gentile, as you Saints define the term."

The Mormon elder cum lawman didn't bat an eye as he replied, "It was my understanding that that sutler out at Fort Douglas was an apostate member of that Temple Lot cult. I mean the poor girl no disrespect, but we would hardly call her a Saint. That gang cracked a safe while they were at it, didn't they?"

Longarm didn't ask who, out of all the soldiers, dependents, and civilian employees coming in to town over the past few days, might have spread the word. He smiled thinly and said, "They didn't crack it. At least one of them had the combination. Seeing you already know so many military secrets, they sent for me to keep from calling on you or your territorial guard for help. They thought you all might get excited about that victim who was supposed to be a Mormon, and I suspect they're embarrassed about the situation getting that far out of hand before the officers in charge knew a thing about it. It seems that a wicked schoolmarm corrupted three or four of her students and a trio of enlisted men without any of the many officers that should have noticed it noticing it. They'd have likely been playing slap and tickle in the cellar of the post schoolhouse this evening if Miss Petula hadn't commenced to complain in writing. The gang found out what she'd done before the IG got around to asking the corps commander what was going on right under his nose. Then, when the wild kids suspected the jig was up, they were able to burn any evidence at the school along with the one who seemed willing to bear witness against them, help themselves to traveling money whilst everybody who should have been watching Corps Headquarters was watching the post engineers fight the fire, and ride off post on seven stolen mounts without being challenged. I was able to ride off post this very evening without being challenged, and that was *after* such a wild night!''

The Mormon police chief looked sort of smug, and confirmed some of Major Sullivan's concerns about unwanted publicity when he chuckled and said, ''They were just as butter-fingered when they were sent out here to tame us back in fifty-seven. After some . . . outlaws cut off and captured three wagon trains carrying army supplies, they told us they'd won and set up camp over a hard day's ride to the southeast of our capital here. They didn't have the nerve to set up Fort Douglas, close enough for any . . . sympathizers to get at, until Washington had sued for peace.''

Longarm had heard the story a little differently. It likely depended on one's point of view. He had no call to argue ancient history. He knew he'd never in this world get any Mormon to admit that those first 2500 troopers had been mauled on orders of the Salt Lake Temple by anybody. So there was no point in describing the culprits as Destroying

Angels, Mormon guerrillas, or big speckled birds.

He said, "I'd be obliged if you all could cordon off that double murder soon as possible and help me scout it and the surrounding sagebrush as soon as it's light enough. I have to catch some sleep, and Lord only knows when I'd be free to ride back if I rode back to Fort Douglas in the wee small hours with those horses and news about that boy and an officer's wife!"

The police chief said Longarm and the two ponies were welcome to bunk with them right there until morning, and suggested, "Wouldn't it be more considerate if we sent a messenger out to Fort Douglas after they've blown Assembly? That way anyone who'd like to join us at those tract houses closer to town would have a full night's sleep and some breakfast under their belts."

Longarm agreed, and that was how they did it. He caught close to four hours of sleep in an empty jail cell in the back. The bunk was comfortable enough, once they loaned him plenty of extra blankets for padding and left the bars unlocked.

The desk sergeant woke him as they were changing shifts and the day crew was having donuts and buttermilk in the wardroom. Longarm was dying for some coffee and a smoke, but the chocolate glazing on the home-baked donuts helped him wake up some. The chief of police and a brace of Salt Lake City detectives he hadn't met before showed up just as he'd about finished. The chief said he'd already sent word out to the fort along with both ponies that belonged there. So Longarm borrowed a handsome Morgan cordovan gelding with a police McClellan saddle from their own remuda, and they rode back out to the murder scene.

The unsold house had been surrounded by rope strung between stakes pounded into the weed-and-debris-scattered property lines. Mormon lawmen in navy-blue uniforms and billed caps stood guard on all four sides. A civilian working for the contractor who'd just built all those houses had ridden out with a key to the front door. So it stood open to the crisp morning air. The Great Basin, or basin-and-range country, that lay between the Rockies and the Sierra Nevadas along the California line tended to have colder nights and warmer days than you'd expect at any season because of its general altitude and usually clear skies.

So both the cadavers inside lay waxen-faced in full rigor, while that warm smell of mingled blood and piss had faded, to be replaced by the distinctive odors of a new house nobody had lived in long enough for things to smell more homey.

Both Indians and Chinese had assured Longarm that they could always tell when white folks lived in a place. He'd assured them that *they* smelled sort of different too.

One of the Mormon detectives hunkered down to examine the dead woman. He was too bright to touch anything, but observant enough to say, "Shot in the back. This big ugly hole in the front of her duster was the exit wound."

His partner, closer to the dead boy, said, "This one was shot from the front, close range, judging by the powder burns. Try it this way. He was surprised by somebody he trusted. He still has a Harrington and Richardson target pistol stuck in his waistband. There's no sign of any struggle, and he fell backwards like a tree sawed off at the stump with both hands down at his sides."

Longarm glanced back at the dead woman. One of the hands she'd tried to unbutton his fly with the night before was level with her handsome gold ear bob, close to her dead features. He nodded and said, "That works pretty good. When I first got here last night she was still soft and warm. He'd been dead a spell already. Let's say somebody found out he'd been meeting, or agreed to meet, his dear old momma here. She told me earlier he wanted to surrender. Let's say they didn't want anybody who knew that much about them surrendering to any law. So they just up and gunned him, say just after dark, and then waited quite a spell until she drove in to run him home or work out some agreement for him to come in on his own."

The police chief stroked his graying beard thoughtfully before he decided, "Seems awfully cold-blooded. But both the method and motive hold together well. You can see at a glance nobody was out to rape or rob this handsome woman. You say she managed a scream of dismay as they were killing her, Deputy Long?"

Longarm shook his head and replied, "I doubt she ever knew what hit her. She'd have let out that holler when she found her boy dead on the floor in here. Then she was shot betwixt the shoulder blades at close range. The hydrostatic shock would have frozen her heart and spine long enough to drop her whether the bullet passed directly through either or not."

He looked away, muttering that was likely just as well, as he saw a white man dressed sort of like an Indian and an Indian dressed sort of like a white man coming in the front door.

The police chief introduced them as a market hunter and his Paiute tracker. Nobody ever introduced *any* well-armed Mormon without a steady job as a Danite. Longarm figured the hunter might have been what they said he was when the man said, "Two ponies, shod U.S. Army Remount style. They left the road two houses to the south and circled in to be tethered out back to a yard pump. They were left there long enough to get fretful. Somebody put out a dishpan of water, but they still tried to bust loose a lot. So they were left there a cruel amount of time. Then they ran off with one in the lead and the other close behind, to the north this time, and circled back to the road where one fool hoofprint looks like any other."

Longarm asked, "What about the army-shod pony I tethered off to the south last night, or the carriage pony I found here?"

The Indian looked disgusted and said, "Nobody asked us to read *that* sign. But hear me. After you ran back to your own mount on foot, you rode it here and then you left with both horses, straight across the front yard to the road."

Longarm asked, "Did you notice any other heel marks out yonder?"

The Mormon market hunter said, "You were the only one running. The dirt's soft enough to hold hoofprints and pounding heel marks. If we're discussing whether the riders of those other brutes left footprints in the sunbaked patches between the weeds, they never did. The way we read it, two riders rode in last night and one rider rode out, leading a pony a hundred pounds or so lighter on its feet going than coming. If that ties in with anything in here, so be it. If it don't, so be it. We call the shots as they pepper the target."

That sounded fair to Longarm. One of the detectives came down the stairs from the second floor holding a pair of frilly female pantaloons.

He said, "Look what I just found up in the front bedroom. They left empty food cans, liquor bottles, and a revolting pile of tobacco butts up there as well. It looks as if our murderous Gentile runaways spent at least one night holed up in this house."

The police chief took the unmentionables and held them up to the light before he grimaced. "They were holed up indeed, with at least this one woman. There's no blood. Just this crotch left stiff as cardboard. So it's anyone's guess whether they wouldn't give them back to her or she just didn't want them anymore."

One of the detectives soberly volunteered, "From the gossip making the rounds about that wicked schoolmarm, she'd have little call to put her pantaloons back on between times. Say she just put them on that first night to ride astride, after one of those orgies . . ."

The police chief made a wry face and set the evidence aside on one windowsill for the time being as they all heard hoofbeats outside and moved over toward the front door.

What had just ridden in was Major Sullivan and a mounted squad of his military police, all nine of them looking mad as wet hens.

When he spotted Longarm in the doorway with all those

Mormon lawmen, Sullivan blazed, "What's going on over here? What's the meaning of all this, Deputy Long? Have you disobeyed my direct orders, damn your eyes?"

To which Longarm could only reply, "Had to. To begin with, I ain't in your army and you ain't in position to direct me to shit. After that, we may or may not have federal jurisdiction here. Come inside and tell us whether we just found Bobby Worthington and his mother dead or whether we have us a worse mystery on our hands."

Sullivan dismounted, handed his reins to a bemused Mormon copper badge who didn't work for him either, and stomped inside to take one look and bitch, "Jesus, Mary, and Joseph, they really did kill the wife and stepson of our Captain Bradford! I was hoping there might be some mistake, or a ruse, when they told me you were the one who'd reported a double murder to the Salt Lake Temple!"

Longarm gently pointed out, "I never reported nothing to any Salt Lake Temple. I reported it to the Salt Lake City police. That's the law. I had no choice."

Major Sullivan whirled on him to snap, "The hell you say! I told you *not* to involve any local lawmen in our private military affairs. Since I see you can't be trusted to follow simple orders, and since you just told me in front of everyone here that you feel no duty to obey my orders, you are off the case. Thank you very much for all you've done to muddy the waters further, and you can haul your insubordinate ass out of my sight now."

He struck a pose to add, "If you don't think I have authority to give you direct orders, just wait and see what happens when I order my men to arrest you if you're still in this corps area after sundown!"

Chapter 14

Longarm knew Major Sullivan was an old pal of his boss, Marshal Vail, who impressed him somewhat more. So he gently suggested it was time for a private conversation, and the major was smart enough to go back to the empty kitchen area with him. So Longarm didn't have to tell the older man to go fuck himself in front of all those Mormons he was so afraid of looking bad in front of.

When the officer repeated his threat in private, Longarm replied in a kinder but no softer tone, "Bullshit. This ain't Texas under the Army of Reconstruction, and even if it was, you're not talking to a defeated Rebel or even a Mormon who fought you to a draw. You're talking to a paid-up federal lawman, and before you put your foot in your mouth about three dead civilians from Fort Douglas, I have been personally shot at more than once, and I sure as shit have the authority to work on *that* case. If you want me to check my rifle and stuff out of your BOQ out yonder and work from a hotel here in town, I will. If you want to go on hogging everything you find out about that schoolmarm and her frisky gang, so be it. But you'd sure be going about it dumb. Thanks to my sharing some of the glory with those lawmen out front who had the jurisdiction, I've already found out some things neither you nor me knew shit about last night.''

The provost marshal grudgingly asked what else Longarm had learned.

Longarm said, ''These regular Salt Lake Mormons already knew about that Temple Lot sutler's daughter, and yet they never got excited about it. The kids who killed her had noticed this tract of empty houses while riding back and forth from town, and used this one as their first hideout whilst they scouted around for a better one. That means they had to have moved in to the second one recently. They might have used some of that money they rode off with to work something out with somebody who wasn't in on the crimes out to the fort. Such folks are prone to turn outlaws in for more money if they know there's a bounty on them.''

Major Sullivan grimaced and said, ''The War Department would never go for that. My orders are to hush the story up, not to post any public notices about it!''

Longarm shrugged and said, ''I've noticed there's always three ways to do anything. There's the right way, the wrong way, and the army way. But just in case there's some reason, how come Fort Douglas keeps trying to hush this fool case up when it seems the whole world already knows about it? Those Saints out front had already heard tell of the arson, murder, and robbery. The gunslicks who tried to stop me in Rawlins and Ogden before I could get here must have heard something about my being sent for and—''

''How do you know?'' the army lawman cut in. ''Doesn't it seem odd to you that a sex-mad schoolmarm and a bunch of dirty young boys would be in league with really professional killers?''

Longarm shrugged and replied, ''Those naughty children have killed three people for certain, which is more than those three gunslicks I met up with can say, assuming they were as professional as we suspect they were. We're just guessing about their pasts. I'm hoping the one who calls himself Mike Smith might tell us more. Meanwhile, we don't know that much more about those three deserters and the remaining schoolboys, Callahan and Kraft. Any one of the five could have met up with hired guns in the past, and we know they have the wherewithal to hire guns. It's been said, though I'm sure it could never be true, that a good many outlaws have been known to join the U.S. Army suddenly, as a means to avoid rougher duty turning big rocks into little ones in a prison quarry.''

Sullivan said, ''They only rode off with eighteen hundred dollars. If we assume they shared it evenly . . .''

''They didn't,'' Longarm replied. ''Had that dead boy out in the front room been given two hundred fifty in pocket jingle, it should have taken him longer to get homesick. His momma told me he'd told her he wanted to give up after little more than a week of staying up as late as he liked and sharing one sloppy pussy with five others. Whether she's the leader or taking orders from another mastermind, the wanton ways of that one gal they're sharing seems to be the main thing holding the gang together. Somebody's been doling that money out less generously. You can send for your average gunslick with a hundred or so down and a promise. They generally expect five hundred to a thousand at the end of the dance. So let's say somebody tied up six hundred dollars with that, and paid out another hundred in rent.''

''What do you think they've rented,'' Sullivan demanded, ''a mansion with servants? You can rent a dumbbell flat in New York City for no more than fifteen dollars a month, with running water!''

Longarm said. ''Outlaws ain't as worried about water as much as privacy, and the sort of landlords they have to deal with know it. Salt Lake City may be getting big, but it don't have too many transient visitors. They have to be holed up in some part of town where the neighbors don't run to the Mormon powers that be about at least five boys living with one gal. They could have sold those seven good cavalry mounts for more cash and . . .''

''How do you know they're anywhere in town?'' the

army man demanded. "They'd need those horses if they were hiding out up in the hills to the east or out on the desert to the west, wouldn't they?"

Longarm patiently replied, "Sure, if they'd left Salt Lake City to hole up out in the bushes where they'd be easier to spot. If they'd just been smart enough to divide the damned money, split up near the railroad depot, and go their own ways to anywhere else, we wouldn't be having this conversation. Nobody would have had any call to kill Bobby Worthington and his mother if they'd already left the scene of the crime. I know they *should* have. I wish I could be sure why they've been sticking together. The only reason I can come up with sounds disgusting. One gal can show two or three men a good time at once. It commences to sound tedious as well as distasteful as soon as you're talking about forming a line. That might hold a bunch of randy kids together for a wild party or more. But it's been over a week since they rode off with that one gal, and it ain't as if none of them had ever enjoyed her favors up until then."

He reached absently for a smoke, remembered where they were, and added with a reflective sigh, "She must be one hell of a lay. Bobby Worthington had gotten enough of it. Others could be wavering. There ain't that much honor among thieves, and we could still get us a break if they've already started to fight among themselves. So are you still in or do you want me to just work with the Salt Lake City police and let you know how things turn out?"

Major Sullivan growled, "You don't give a man much choice. I'll bet you spent a lot of time on company punishment when you were in this man's army during the war."

Longarm shrugged and said, "I disremember which army I rode with when me and this old world were more young and foolish. But you're right about company punishment. I don't know what it is about you officers, but it seemed every time I turned around I was walking a tour with full pack or peeling spuds with a dull knife. I'll come out to the post later or send for my own stuff at your BOQ. First I aim to set up closer to that bunch in a downtown hotel. I have a police mount at my disposal in the unlikely event we discover they've made a break for the open range. I'm more likely than you to hear about that first if any Mormon country folks report their passing. How come the army was dumb enough to camp way off to the southwest with all these Mormons across the lines of communication through the mountains to the northeast?''

Sullivan snorted. ''I was not in command. I take all my orders from officers of higher rank. I have to. I can tell you that there are things about this case more complicated than you seem to feel they are. So why not save us both a lot of needless trouble with our own superiors and just trot on back to Denver like a sport?''

Longarm said he'd head back to Denver when he cracked the case or when his own boss told him to let the crooks win. They didn't shake on that. They just rejoined the others and Longarm declared their war over. None of the Mormons asked the major's opinion. They'd all taken part in, or at least heard a lot about, that undeclared and never-resolved Mormon War of '57.

By this time a photographer the Salt Lake law used for such chores had driven out to the scene of the crime, and Longarm watched as they took a lot of photographs from different angles. Major Sullivan said he wanted to take the two bodies back to Fort Douglas with him. Longarm let the chief of police tell him he couldn't have them before their own county coroner held an inquest and released them to their next of kin—not the military police, who had no jurisdiction in the case he was investigating, if it was all the same with them.

Longarm left them still fussing about it as he went out to that police mount and headed into town. He'd visited the City of the Saints many a time before, and knew a good hotel near the railroad depot. It got easier to order coffee or even beer as you got further from the ten prim acres of Temple Square in the center of town.

Things were run stricter in Salt Lake City than they were up in Ogden. But most Mormons were pragmatic as well as saintly, and tolerated what had to be tolerated in the communications center of the basin-and-range country everyone else had to cross to get across the continent.

Some Saints as well as many of their enemies hated to admit it. But the California Gold Rush of '49 would have been far tougher to manage if Mormon way stations hadn't been there to aid and abet the overland wagons. Salt Lake City merchants and a lot of others had prospered as the Pony Express, telegraph lines, the overland stage, and then the iron horse had followed those first wagons west. So unless you'd read those travel books or heard other preachers fussing about the heathen ways of the sinister Saints, a visitor just stretching his legs around the Salt Lake City Railroad Depot could easily take the neighborhood for downtown Denver, Kansas City, or Saint Louis. Most big towns of the time were commencing to look much the same in and around the train stations.

As an experienced lawman with a trained eye for details, Longarm did notice there were no spitoons or ashtrays in the lobby as he entered, but the paper palm trees grew much the same as they did in other such oak-paneled lobbies all across the land.

The portly room clerk knew him from his last visit. But Longarm paid in advance for a corner room and bath upstairs because all his baggage was out at Fort Douglas and he'd seen no sense in paying for stable and tackroom privileges when he could leave his borrowed mount and saddle at the nearby police headquarters.

He held off on wiring his home office at a nickel a word until he had more from the coroner's office about the two latest deaths. Once he'd been assured Bobby Worthington and his mother had been shot just about the way things had looked, with the flattened round of an army-issue .45 dug out of the dead boy's chest from where it had flattened against bone, he sent a progress report to Billy Vail. Then

111

he wired the law up in Ogden to see whether that mysterious Mike Smith had offered to sing louder.

The tight-mouthed son of a bitch hadn't killed anybody for the wicked schoolmarm and her pupils as yet. Unless he was wanted seriously in other parts, he was either stupid or more loyal than most crooks. It was possible he'd bought the myth that the law couldn't hold you more than seventy-two hours on no more than suspicion. That worked when you had a lawyer who knew where you were being held. When lawmen who knew their onions didn't want to turn you loose, they could move you from one city precinct or small-town jail to another, if only to keep you from feeling crowded or uncomfortable on used bedding. Longarm's pals up in Ogden knew the man they were holding had to be guilty of something, and they weren't about to let him out before they found out what it was, or before the rascals he was working for got a mighty expensive lawyer to a Utah judge who'd be willing to take the side of a Gentile outlaw against Mormon lawmen and their pals.

He ate his noon dinner in the railroad terminal, where they looked the other way and served coffee.

Sort of.

You had to know what coffee tasted like to brew it right. But he'd had worse on many a cattle drive, and they were willing to sell him his own brand of cheroots at the news-stand in the waiting room—from under the counter, as if it had been a dirty book.

Longarm asked the Mormon dealer if they had any copies of *Justine* or even *Unhappy Valley*. But the dealer didn't know what he was talking about. He tried a few other places in the seedier parts of town on the other side of the railroad yards. He was offered some bawdy French postcards, and a book by Miss Virginia Woodhull that would have been considered filthy in Denver, seeing she advocated free love as well as voting and full property rights for all women. But he could see Zenobia Lowell and her depraved students had shopped somewhere else.

112

It was possible she'd ordered the books by mail, seeing that at least one member of her gang had driven the mail ambulance and could have kept a transaction like that discreet. Longarm considered letting the postal inspectors in on a possible case of sending pornography through the U.S. mails. But he wasn't certain, and there already were enough spoons in the same broth. So he decided to hold off on that for now.

By this time the little sleep he'd had the night before was catching up on him. So he went back to his hotel to steal a nap while things were slow. He'd kept his room key on him, knowing a room clerk who wanted to jump up and hand you your key every time you came in was either new at the game or a born pain in the ass.

So when he was called over to the desk, he came patting his side pocket and saying, "I got my key right here. Thanks just the same."

But the room clerk said, "That lady you were expecting said she'd come on official business and didn't want someone to know she'd been calling on you here. I had the bellboy run her upstairs with a passkey. I hope that was the right way to handle the situation."

Longarm said, "So do I. Did this lady who said I was expecting her give you a name? What did she look like?"

The clerk replied, "She said she was a Miss Lowell. I'd say she was in her late twenties or early thirties, with a slender build and light brown hair. Do you mean to say you *weren't* expecting her?"

To which Longarm could only reply, "Not here at this hotel. I've been looking for her. I wasn't expecting her to come looking for me! You say she's waiting upstairs in my hired room?"

The clerk said that was about the size of it. So Longarm headed up the stairwell, and didn't draw his gun until he'd reached the second landing.

Chapter 15

The long hallway at the top of the stairs was only illuminated by small windows down at the far ends. So Longarm could make out another pencil line of daylight as he approached his hired room. Someone had left the door ajar, as if hesitant to make themselves too much at home, or to have him in their sights as he sashayed in. So he hugged the wall and eased forward on the balls of his feet, then dropped to one knee by the door with his head below regular waist level and his .44-40 held high.

Then he gently shoved with his free hand, and the door swung open on silent hinges, Lord love the maintenance staff.

But his visitor was standing over by the front windows with her back to him, either unaware of him or a damned fine actress, as she peered down at the street through the cotton lace curtains. She'd tossed a travel-soiled white duster and her sunbonnet over the writing table on that side of the room. So he could see her upswept hair was taffy brown and she was built smaller and more womanly than big blond Frida under her summerweight frock of chocolate calico with vanilla polka dots. He warned himself not to think about the way gals were built when he was fixing to run one in. He rose to his feet and lowered his six-gun, but

114

hung on to it just the same as he said, "Afternoon, Miss Zenobia."

The gal started like a spooked deer and whirled to face him wild-eyed. She was not the gal he'd seen in that photograph of Zenobia Lowell. Before he could say so she said, "You're talking about my big sister, good sir. I'd be Minerva Lowell, and you can't think poor Zenobia hurt anybody! You can't! You can't!"

To which Longarm gently but firmly replied, "Sure I can. The dead bodies are piling up like it's the last act of *Hamlet*, and if your big sister ain't in on it, it's about time she came forward and explained a heap of things. So where's she at, Miss Minerva?"

The younger and in truth better-looking of the Lowell gals heaved a great sigh and said, "If only I knew. About a week ago she wired me for emergency funds, saying she was in a terrible fix and had to get home to Boston right away. I wired her two hundred dollars. It was as much as I wanted to trust her with. Zenobia would never hurt a fly, but she tends to have a lot of emergencies and never remembers to pay me back."

Longarm said, "We all have kith and kin like that. Let's not worry about how much you might have sent. Where did you send it and then what happened, Miss Minerva? Might they ever call you Minny, by the way?"

She wrinkled her nose and said, "I wish you wouldn't. Zenobia asked me to wire her in care of Western Union here in Salt Lake City. When I visited them earlier, their records showed my money order had been signed for and cashed the morning after it arrived. I'd included a message to wire back collect and tell me what was going on. She never did. Then I wired Fort Douglas to see if they could tell me anything, and that's when I learned my big sister was missing and suspected of murder and worse!"

Longarm shut the door behind him with his heel and holstered his .44-40 as he assured her, "Nothing's worse than murder, and there ain't no fate worse than death. A body

115

can get over most anything else in time, but once you've killed somebody, they won't ever forgive you.''

The younger of the Lowell gals moved closer to him, saying, "My sister couldn't have been party to that school-girl's murder. I caught the next train out of Boston as soon as I heard she'd been implicated in some sort of mischief. I got in to Salt Lake City a little after noon, and thank heavens I went to the police station before I hired a ride out to Fort Douglas! They told me you knew as much about the mess as anybody and that you were staying at this hotel just down the way!''

Longarm waved her to a seat on the bedstead and swung a bentwood chair from the writing table to straddle it as he muttered, "Me and my big mouth. Now that you've found me, what else can you tell me about your sister and those rough playmates she's fallen in with? Did she write you about her advanced classes at the post schoolhouse, and whilst we're on the subject, how come she told the person-nel officer out to Fort Douglas she had a teaching degree when it turns out she don't?''

Minerva Lowell sighed and said, "She means no harm but, well, she fibs a little to get her way. She always has. I suppose you've heard that silly poem about the Lowells of Boston?''

He nodded and recited, " 'Here's to the city of Boston, the land of the bean and the cod, where the Cabots speak only to Lowells and the Lowells speak only to God.' Or is it the other way around?''

She smiled ruefully and replied, "Sometimes they sub-stitute the Lodges for the Cabots. My point is that we're poor relations of the really rich Lowells of Back Bay Bos-ton. But you'd never know that to hear Zenobia go on about our cotton mills. Fibbing about fine schools and spurning the proposals of the lieutenant governor of Massachusetts are mere conversation starters for poor Zenobia. Sometimes I think she believes the stories that seem to pop out of her

116

mouth when there's no reason to lie. You see, she has this condition.''

''I've heard of it,'' Longarm said. ''It's called compulsive lying. I've never understood it either. But there seems to be an old boy in every outfit who's really the missing Dauphin of France or the original inventor of the telegraph, robbed of his rights by the Paris mob or the villainous Sam Morse.''

She shook her head sadly and replied, ''If only things were that simple. When I said Zenobia suffered from a condition, I meant we both inherited this . . . physical condition that's inclined to make a woman . . . excitable. I've learned to cope with it by concentrating on the modest family hardware business we poorer Lowells were left to run. Zenobia has always been more . . . driven. I've told her and told her that there's no golden land of dreams just over the horizon. But she's never been able to sit still, and once she gets somewhere, she's never been able hold on to a job, a beau, or even a pet canary long enough to matter!''

Longarm said, ''Let's talk about beaux. When last heard from, no offense, your big sister was said to have six of them, carrying on mighty sassy in the cellar of that post schoolhouse after hours. Is it your contention the late Petula Dorman was lying about that, and if so, how come they killed her to shut her up?''

Minerva Lowell twisted her hands in her lap and repressed a sob before she replied, ''I wouldn't put a sex orgy past poor Zenobia. As I said, there's this female complaint that runs in our family. But I just can't believe she'd agree to anything criminal!''

Longarm had no call to point out that mass fornication was a felony in more than one state. He followed her drift. Sort of.

He chose his words carefully before he told her, ''If this conversation was taking place in Colorado, we'd be having it with a federal police matron present. I ain't sure my boss in Denver would want me to carry you over to the Salt Lake

City Federal Building. He ordered me to work tight with the military over this way, and I've already had to share the spreading puddle with more lawmen than that. So to save time, and with the understanding that you still have my undivided respect, Miss Minerva, might this physical condition you mentioned be known as *pseudohymenal labia minora*?"

She looked blank, looked away, and replied, "I don't know what an anatomy professor might call it. I only know it leaves a woman who's suffering from it awfully . . . excitable."

Longarm said, "So I've been told. I wish there was a more delicate way to put it, and you ain't going to like my conclusions either way, but that charred body they hauled out of the cellar of that burned-down schoolhouse was suffering, or blessed, with a peculiar condition. They tell me— and so far I've had no reason to doubt it—that the gang left Miss Petula Dorman tied up to die in that fire. I'll be switched with snakes if I can see why a wicked schoolgal would accuse an innocent schoolmarm of being a sex fiend and then murder her, but I've never led a gang of sex fiends."

He took a deep breath, let half of it out so his voice wouldn't crack, and said, "I know this is an unusual request, and I want you to recall I was seated over here with the back of this chair betwixt our private parts when and if you'd be good enough to show me exactly what you mean by a physical condition you share with your missing sister, ma'am."

She stared at him thunderstruck. "Are you asking to see my pussy?"

To which Longarm could only reply, "Yes, ma'am, in the name of the law and for strictly investigative reasons. It could save us hours of guessing if I knew for a fact which of two different gals might be the one still alive and riding with that gang, and vice versa."

So Minerva Lowell blushed even redder than before, and stood up to hoist her skirts and drop her pantaloons down around her ankles. Then she stepped out of them and sat back on the bed, closer to the middle, and raised her knees and hooked her high heels on the edge of the mattress before she murmured, "Please be gentle," and lay back to spread her pale smooth thighs wide.

Longarm stared soberly at the mighty tempting but otherwise ordinary-looking groove parting the light brown hair between her legs, which were sheathed in expensive silk stockings below the bare knees, and took another deep breath before he asked in a desperately calm voice, "Could I have just one peek inside, ma'am?"

She sort of moaned, and reached down with both hands to part the lips and expose her pink wet gash to the light and his admiring view.

Her clit was engorged and those inner lips were inflamed, but after that her old ring-dang-doo just looked . . . swell. She didn't have that false cherry Nurse Ericsson and the body she and Doc Sloan had looked into, literally, had had.

So Longarm soberly told Minerva Lowell, "The good news is that your sister would seem to be still alive. The bad news is that she's still wanted in connection with murder, arson, and robbery."

She didn't seem to be paying him any mind.

Longarm said, "I wish you wouldn't do that, ma'am," as she went right on playing with herself, with two fingers probing her otherwise natural-looking opening while a third strummed her old banjo.

She moaned, "I can't help myself at times like these. I promised myself I wouldn't lose control this time, but the thought of a handsome man in the same room with me alone, staring right into my very being in broad daylight, just got me too excited. Why don't you take off your own pants and join me, you fool?"

Longarm smiled sheepishly, but kept his elbows on the back of the bentwood chair he straddled with his own excitement throbbing in his tobacco-tweed pants as he soberly replied, "I'd be lying, and you'd know I was lying, if I said

119

I wasn't mighty tempted, ma'am. But I'm on duty at the moment and I told you I only aimed to examine some . . . evidence.''

She didn't answer as she commenced to move her hips up and down in time with her own finger-fucking. Longarm knew he'd be in just as much trouble if he whipped his old organ-grinder out and jacked off in time with her. He could just see himself addressing the judge. "If it please the court, I never stuck it all the way in the accused. We just jacked off together whilst I was questioning her.''

He was hoping she'd never wind up the accused. He had no call to doubt the story she'd just given him. She could probably prove she'd been back East in Boston during all those scandalous or criminal doings out to Fort Douglas, and surely Billy Vail would understand a gentleman was supposed to help an innocent lady in distress.

She didn't sound like a lady as she pleaded, "Come over here and mount me like a man! I know I'm acting like a slut! I can't *help* acting like a slut once someone gets me started, and it was your idea, not mine, you cruel and heartless beast!''

Longarm was reminded of that joke about a true sadist being kind to a masochist. He didn't say so. He knew anything he said was likely to excite her more. She'd just told him it had made her feel dirty to be alone in the room with a man. He idly wondered if she might not be getting a bigger thrill out of him just watching her jack off than she would if he took her up on her kind offer. Both de Sade and von Sacher Masoch had published mighty queer suggestions about such matters, and she'd said her warm nature ran in her family.

She cursed him again and moaned, "I'm almost there, but I need some help here! Won't you even put a finger in me, kind sir?''

That sounded like a more reasonable request, astride a chair with a raging erection, than it was likely to sound in court if he ever had to explain this unseemly situation. He knew he was going to come out just as silly to some of the jury whether he admitted under oath he'd taken advantage of a material witness in a capital case or sat there like a big-ass bird watching her play with herself like that!

He'd had similar silent arguments with himself trying to cut down on other bad habits. He knew he smoked too much and wasn't supposed to drink with Indians, but common sense was one thing and natural feelings were another.

So there was no telling how things might have turned out that afternoon in his hired room if there hadn't come a pounding on the door to the hall. It sounded urgent.

Longarm didn't have to tell a Lowell from Boston to behave her fool self as he rose to his feet and called, "I'm coming! Who is it?"

Minerva was sitting up primly with her hands folded in her lap and her skirts down as a voice from outside called back, "Roundsman Lee of the Salt Lake City police. They sent me to fetch you, Deputy Long!"

Longarm opened the door wide to ask the young copper badge in blue what they wanted of him over to their headquarters.

Roundsman Lee said, "Chief's compliments and that gang from Fort Douglas seems to have broken cover. Five men and one woman just stopped the Skull Valley stage just west of the city limits. They robbed the passengers and busted into the U.S. mails looking for more. So the chief says we have to cut your local federal lawmen in for the chase. He sent me to tell you you're welcome to tag along if you'd care to be in on the kill!"

Chapter 16

The feeder line that served Salt Lake City ran trains down the Mormon Delta as far as Marysvale, but there were barely wagon ruts to follow around the south shore of the Great Salt Lake and then off the more beaten tracks toward the remote Mormon settlement and Indian agency at Skull Valley. Hardly anyone but Mormons would have bothered.

But the Book of Mormon held the American Indians to be members of a lost tribe of Israel, and whether this was true or not, the belief had resulted in the white settlers of Deseret, or the Utah Territory, getting along better with Indians than some had in other parts. The emigrant and overland trails most covered wagons and the later Pony Express and railroads had followed swung *north* of the Great Salt Lake for the sensible reason that the going was rougher around the south shores. *Some* westbound greenhorns had taken it, that most unfortunate Donner party being the most notorious example.

The mail route to Skull Valley led southwest into even bleaker basin-and-range country, with the agency and the settlement that fed it near the headwaters of a seasonal wash running north toward the lake across flat desert in the wind shadow of the Cedar Mountains, a long low range that wasn't half as green as its name might suggest. Scrub cedar and pinyon pine could grow on less than ten inches of rain a year, and in the Cedar Mountains, that was as much as they usually got.

Nobody was talking about riding half that far that afternoon, of course. The Skull Valley Agency was a five- or six-hour ride from the city, and the robbery had taken place much closer, just after the coach had made its last relay stop at Kearns, around ten miles out.

As Longarm rode out along the coach road on another borrowed police mount with Lee and another copper badge, he saw Minerva Lowell chasing after them, sidesaddle, on a livery roan mare. So seeing it was about time for a trail break, he reined in under the shade of some apple trees the Mormons at a nearby farm had planted alongside the road. The copper badges did the same, further down the road, when they saw he wanted to wait for that wild-riding gal in the white duster and sunbonnet.

As she reined in beside him, Longarm said, "You can't come with us, Miss Minerva. We're riding to join armed and dangerous men on the prod for at least one strange woman on a horse. Having you along could complicate things for us and be distressful for you. We're sure hoping to round up them wild kids alive, but—"

"It's my sister and a free country along a public right-of-way!" she declared. "If anyone can reason with poor Zenobia, I can. I refuse to believe she could be the leader of the gang. But whether she is or not, I've always been able to calm her down when she's had one of her starts."

Longarm said, "I was wondering what you called them. All right. If I can't make you stay out of it, make sure you stick tight as a tick to me. For like I said, one of the stage robbers has been described as a handsome young gal with light brown hair."

Roundsman Lee walked his own mount back to ask how long Longarm was likely to just sit there. Longarm glanced at the sky and replied they'd best move it on to where the action might be.

So they did. They soon came to a whole remuda of ponies tethered in another apple orchard under empty saddles. Longarm whistled thoughtfully as he saw the long picket line of dismounted riders in outfits ranging from cow to blue police uniforms, all armed with rifles or shotguns as they faced southwest along the weed-grown fence lines, which ran clean out of sight.

An older man Longarm recalled from the Salt Lake City Federal Court came out on the dusty road with his Winchester cradled over an arm as he stared coldly up at Longarm and declared, "It was so good of you to deal us in on this case, Denver boy. Now that we're in, you're out. So why don't you run home and tell Billy Vail he ought to be ashamed of himself?"

Longarm smiled down at Vail's angry opposite number from the Salt Lake City office. "Wasn't his notion, or even mine, Marshal. The provost marshal out to Fort Douglas was anxious to keep the noise down to a roar."

The Mormon federal marshal snapped, "I'd tell you what I think of that Major Sullivan if there wasn't a lady present and the Book of Mormon didn't forbid such language. I sent a rider for him. Not that he and his soldiers blue deserve the time of day from me, but because we can use all the help we can get over this way. I've taken charge of this full federal and local *posse comitatus*. We can argue about trial jurisdiction after we've caught the rascals. Are we going to have any argument about that, *Deputy* Long?"

To which Longarm felt obliged to reply, "Not from this child. You got me outgunned as well as outranked. But could I ask you how far we might be from the scene of that holdup, Marshal?"

The Mormon sounded more mollified as he told Longarm, "About a mile and a half out. They popped out of some roadside chaparral as the stage was topping a rise and naturally rolling slow. Our witnesses say they behaved wilder than your average road agents. So nobody resisted until they'd ransacked everything and everybody to mount up and ride off like a bunch of young cowboys shooting up a trail town. The shotgun messenger got off a parting shot with the ten-gauge he'd held in reserve under his seat. He thinks he might have winged one of them. So do we. Our Paiute trackers found the spot where they turned off the road for a spell. There was blood all around. They probably changed their clothes there and rode back onto the road to proceed at a more stately pace.''

Longarm frowned thoughtfully and said, "That's the way it's often done, sir. But how come you're set up so close to the scene of the crime, no offense? Is there some natural law forbidding them to have ridden on into town, or anywhere else, long before you could have heard from anybody aboard that coach?''

The older lawman stared up narrow-eyed. "Is that why they sent for one Colorado Gentile instead of calling on me, mine, and some pretty fair Indian trackers? Do they really think we spend all our time at prayer meetings or kidnapping wagon-train girls for those dreadful white slave markets out in those secret canyons? We know they haven't ridden past here because those farm folks yonder have neither gone blind nor seen hide nor hair of the gang this afternoon!''

Longarm glanced across the road and through some trees to where a couple of women in sunbonnets were serving grub to possemen at a trestle table in front of their farmhouse.

He nodded and pointed out, "You were the one who just said they'd ridden off the road to change clothes, bleed, or whatever.''

The marshal insisted, "I said they'd ridden *back* to the road. They would have left other sign for our Indians to read if they'd tried to circle across country over unirrigated desert pavement or cultivated fields. The way our Indians read it, the gang must have loped just out of sight, waited off the road until the coach drove on into town to spread the alarm, then ridden back to the road, where their tracks would be lost among all the others, and then doubled back, still in a bunch or strung out, to appear less memorable."

Longarm pursed his lips and decided, "I follow your drift. I take it you have trackers out scouting for any turnoffs this side of . . . where?"

The man who knew the country better said, "Kearns, where the coaches headed this way change teams for the last time and where a close-knit church community gathers for business, shopping, and worship. That gang would need nerves of steel and a lot of luck to ride through Kearns. If they left the road to hide or circle, they'll have left sign for our trackers to read. If they stay on the road, our advance scouts will catch them on it. In sum, we're talking about less than a dozen miles they can bounce back and forth along without leaving tracks, and even as we speak that road to nowhere is getting shorter under them!"

Longarm asked how much money the gang had gotten away with this time. The marshal grimaced and said, "Less than three hundred to split six ways. That's a heap of prison time to risk for the money an honest cow hand could ride off with at the end of the month with a clear conscience. I swear, I don't know why so many youngsters just can't see that!"

Longarm shrugged and said, "Lazy, I reckon." He turned to Minerva to say, "The two hundred you sent your sister, the three hundred they just got at gunpoint, and the eighteen hundred they stole from Fort Douglas add up to twenty-three hundred dollars, and they've been on the owlhoot trail less than two weeks. Honest men are raising families on one to three dollars a day. Somebody seems to be spending like a drunken sailor where you can hardly buy liquor, good coffee, or smokes!"

The Mormon marshal asked, "What about somethig stronger? You Gentiles would know better than us about opium or hashish."

Longarm nodded soberly and said, "You're right. Either would be way easier to come by cheaper here in Utah Territory. You can buy all the laudanum you'd ever want in any drugstore.''

The lawman, forbidden any drugs or stimulants, looked puzzled. The lady from Boston explained, ''That's a tincture of opium and alcohol. It's taken for female complaints or given to cranky babies who've started teething.''

Longarm pointed at the farm gals serving refreshments over by that house, and suggested they rest their mounts and wet their whistles. So they rode over and dismounted. The farm gals, all about the same age and likely the wives or daughters of the man of the house, were handing out corn-meal cakes and mugs of buttermilk on tin plates. When Longarm asked how much he owed them, the older sister, or wife, told him not to act as if he was some prince being served by poor people. So he said he was sorry, and she told him to just make sure he rinsed both plates off at the yard pump along with those buttermilk mugs when they were done with them.

Some smaller farm kids came over to ask if they could water the two ponies and feed them some love grass. Longarm didn't insult them. He just told them they'd be much obliged.

So he and Minerva were closer to the road, seated side by side on the grass in the shade of an apple tree, when a whole troop of military police came in, along with a cage wagon for transporting prisoners, led by the optimistic Major Sullivan.

Sullivan spotted Longarm and the girl off the road as he was still on it, talking to the Mormon marshal and some other local lawmen. He said something about it to Lieutenant Hershey, whom Longarm had borrowed that army bay and saddle from. The junior officer rode over to Longarm and Minerva.

As they rose, Hershey ticked his hat brim and declared, ''They have your baggage and Winchester in the prisoner wagon, Deputy Long. The major said to load them aboard when he heard about the stage holdup. He said he was hoping you'd be here. He just told me to tell you to take your blamed belongings and never come back to Fort Douglas again. Might I ask if this young lady would be a . . . Saint?''

Longarm allowed she wasn't, and just introduced her as Miss Minerva, seeing the officers wanted to be so pouty.

Hershey ticked his hat brim down at the gal and confided to Longarm, ''The major's sore about the Mormons horning in on his case.''

Longarm snorted. ''I sent word about that back to the post with your own horse and saddle, Lieutenant. Nobody's horning in on anything all that purely military. Once your deserters and runaway kids commenced to committ murder and armed robbery off post, somebody else was sure to notice. I just got hell from the local federal authority as the thanks I deserved for trying to keep things out at Fort Douglas so private!''

Over on the road, Major Sullivan was staring their way hard. So his junior officer saluted Minerva again and said he had to see what the major wanted.

As he swung the ass of his pony their way, tail high, Minerva asked what all that had been about.

Longarm said, ''Send a man on a fool's errand and he's likely to be treated like a fool. Let's hand these mugs and plates back so I can fetch my own gear before they auction it off.''

As they headed back toward the farmhouse, she asked him what was going to happen next.

Longarm shrugged and said, ''You just heard that shavetail tell me it was out of my hands. The only authority I had this far west came by leave of the provost marshal who just fired me. Neither the federal or local civilian authorities ever asked for my help, and the Salt Lake marshal seems almost as annoyed with me as that puffed-up army major.''

She sounded more upset as she demanded, ''Then who's going to help me find my poor sister Zenobia?''

To which he could only reply, trying to sound gentle, ''I wouldn't worry my pretty little head about that, Miss Minerva. Every man jack you see out this way this afternoon is intent on locating your big sister and all her little playmates. You were there just now when the marshal explained the fix they're in. It won't be dark for hours and the moon's already up, more than half full, with nary a cloud in the sky. They can't follow yonder road to either town at either end of a ten- or twelve-mile stretch. They can't turn off it without leaving a clear trail for the law to follow. They can't stay on it unless they mean to make an alley fight of it in broad daylight. So why don't you just stay put here, and I'm sure they'll be bringing your sister in before sundown, hopefully alive and well, if she's as harmless as you say.''

As he moved to the yard pump with their mugs and plates, she asked where he might be going.

Longarm told her, ''Back to my hotel for some sleep. I barely got four hours last night, and I was already feeling it when you all showed up to haul me out here on another fool's errand. I might feel more like being in on the kill if I was feeling more peppy. On the other hand, I've never really enjoyed Mex bullfights just sitting up in the stands. So I'll let all the local bigwigs argue about who might claim what the Mexicans call the moment of truth, and I'll wire my boss for his permission to come on home after a good night's sleep.''

He ran pump water over the hardware they'd snacked off as Minerva stood there shifting her weight from one foot to the other, like a kid trying not to piss.

Then she said, ''I'm going back to town with you. I don't know anyone else out here I can confide in, and they'll surely tell you as soon as they know anything more about my sister, won't they?''

He sighed and said, ''I'd as soon they wouldn't. But they likely will. Can't you get it through your pretty little head that they've thrown me out of their hunting party, Miss Minerva?''

She demurely replied, ''Of course I can. That's another good reason for me to ride back to that hotel with you, you big silly!''

Chapter 17

Getting back to the city was a chore too tedious to waste much conversation on. He got sort of tired of asking Minerva Lowell to go away and stop pestering him.

When she followed him, his saddlebags, and his Winchester up the stairs of his hotel, he turned on the last landing to demand, "How many times do I have to tell you that I'm off the case, dog-tired, and not interested? Why did you come all the way back to town with me when your sister is still somewhere out yonder and there must be over a hundred men more horny than me along that picket line if the waiting makes you fidgety, Miss Minerva?"

She said, "I don't know any of them. I know you were about to fuck me when we were so rudely interrupted, and I always *have* felt more . . . gushy when I was worried about something. Do you really think they'll catch Zenobia and those boys this evening, Custis?"

He shifted the bulky McClellan he had braced against his hip, and moved on up the stairs as he grunted. "No. They're too sure of themselves, and somebody riding with your sister knows a thing or two about the owlhoot trail. They've been riding it for close to two weeks without leaving sign worth mention. I suspect they scatter betwixt orgies or business meetings and hide out separately. They've left as few hoof marks as possible, and stuck mostly to well-beaten paths where nobody can track 'em. I don't know where they rode when just two of 'em left that tract house to the northwest of here. I've no idea which way they rode after they rallied just off the road after their stage holdup today. I can't see the leader who's been out there calling the shots so far running them up and down an open road like a steam piston either. But like I said, they'd thrown me off the case. So it's their misfortune and none of my own.''

He unlocked the door to his hired room, and she tagged along as he draped his saddle over the foot of the bedstead, Winchester, saddlebags, and all. It was her idea to shut the door and throw the barrel bolt as Longarm put his hat on the dresser and shucked his coat with a bemused smile, saying, "It's only fair to warn you I'm fixing to take off all my duds and get in bed now, Miss Minerva. I know what I told you before about compromising myself as the arresting officer. But I don't see how I'll get to arrest your big sister now."

She said, "Goody!" and tossed her own sunbonnet and purse aside to start unbuttoning her bodice.

Longarm left his own buttons alone as he laughed and said, "Hold on. I was joshing. There's a time and place for everything. But ain't you afraid they'll come pounding on the door again with news about Zenobia?''

Minerva's voice was muffled by folds of calico as she pulled her dress off over her head, saying, "Pooh, she's got her own men to pleasure her, and you just said they're not likely to catch her tonight!''

Longarm's breath caught in mingled desire and distaste. She'd put those frilly pantaloons back on, but she was bare from the belly button up, and put together as if she'd been whittled out of marble by one of those ancient Greek craftsmen to stick in some pagan temple dedicated to some randy goddess.

But she was likely tetched in the head, and surely as shopworn between the legs as her crazy sister. So he told himself

131

that even though he was off the case and hadn't been getting any lately, it wouldn't be smart to mess with this one.

Then Minerva dropped her pantaloons around her ankles and stepped out of them again, diving atop the bedcovers and rolling over with her high heels aimed at opposite ends of the room as she put both hands in her yawning naked lap. "What are you waiting for?" she asked. "Do you mean to make me start ahead of you all by myself again?"

In point of fact he gave her plenty of time to strum her old banjo as he kept telling himself to stop every time he unbuttoned another button. So by the time he was out of his own pants she was starting to come, and it sure felt wild to plunge his raging erection into her throbbing wet warmth as she dug a heel into the mattress edge to either side and thrust right back at him as he took her with his socks on the rug and his arms braced stiff to either side of her writhing torso.

She came again before him, and he came faster than usual in Minerva Lowell, thanks to all that earlier teasing by both her and the late Bobby Worthington's late momma. But once he had come in Minerva hard, it seemed only polite to kiss her, and that seemed to set her off again.

So a grand time was had by all, and he'd gotten over his confused feelings about her by the time they had to stop for a cuddle and smoke lest they pant themselves to death.

He'd noticed before, once he'd busted the ice with a friendly whore, or a gal who'd been earlier with somebody he just didn't like, that it was easier to feel disgusted at a gal's favors to other men before you noticed how good it felt to your own wicked privates.

As they shared a cheroot with her fondling his limp organ-grinder, she started to tell him she wasn't really the kind of a gal she was, or try to tell him. Longarm had never understood why a woman who'd just screwed you wild and free wanted you to think she'd never come before.

He patted her bare shoulder and stuck the cheroot between her lips as he warned, "Don't smear the magic with bullshit, honey. Let's just pretend we're a couple of new-born babes smoking corn silk for the first time in this nursery crib. I don't do this with just anybody I meet back in Denver either.''

He couldn't help adding, ''Only the halfway pretty ones.''

She laughed, and passed back the cheroot as she answered, ''Aren't we just awful? Coming out here on the train, with nobody but this very hand to keep me company in my Pullman berth, I started trying to add up all the lovers I've had, partly for inspiration as I was trying to come, and I fear I still can't decide whether you count another girl you've been silly with the same as a man who failed to satisfy you. Does that sound crazy to you, Custis?''

Longarm felt himself rising to the occasion again as he set the awkward cheroot aside and said, ''Not hardly. Everybody jacks off as they add up their score now and again. You're right about it feeling more inspiring than made-up dream gals. But it's tough to feel sure, once you get past fifty or so, whether you ought to count a one-night stand the same as an all-summer romance. Fortunately, I seldom get silly with other men. So I don't have that particular problem.''

She began to move her hand with more interest as she felt his flesh responding. She sat up to watch what she was doing as she replied with not a hint of embarrassment, ''You ought to try that some time. I didn't think I'd like it until I gave in just to get a better grade from this naughty schoolmarm who kept keeping me after school. She said she hated men and wanted to show me why we didn't need them. She never convinced me I didn't enjoy fucking. But having been licked down there by both genders, I have to say nobody eats pussy like somebody who owns one. I hear nobody can suck cock as good as another man for the same reasons. You have to know what it feels like before you really know how to do it, see?''

Longarm grimaced and replied, ''I reckon. Don't worry. I wasn't too anxious to go down on you to begin with.''

She laughed again, and rolled all the way up on her knees

to pivot and impale her sculpted young torso on his new erection as she told him she'd just have to see if she could suck him off that way.

She could. Once she'd dug a high heel in to either side of his bare hips and began to move up and down fast enough to make her tits flop, it felt as if he was in her for the first time, and better yet, that position reminded him of the way that army wife had spread her thighs across that windowsill twice.

"I'm sure glad they fired me this afternoon," Longarm said as he rolled her over on her own back to brace a stiff arm under each of her upraised knees and pound her the rest of the way to mutual pleasure.

But that last remark turned out to be a tactical mistake, because by now the frisky Minerva felt comfortable enough between her legs to worry a tad more about her big sister.

When he sensed her lack of enthusiasm and asked if she wanted him to stop, she told him to go on and satisfy himself and that she didn't really mind.

Of course, as any man could have told her, and likely had at such times in the past, there was nothing, including a bucket of water or a gun to his head, that could calm a man down faster than telling him to just go on screwing any gal who said she really didn't mind.

So Longarm rolled off with a thin smile and confided, "I met this gal one time who said she'd saved herself from rape with that warm remark. But I sure thank you for those inspiring earlier remarks, and I can see how you'd be more worried about your sister right now."

She followed him into position to snuggle some more with their heads on the pillows as he idly wondered whether to light that cheroot again or not. He decided not to. She snuggled closer, and told him he was so understanding. She reached down absently for the love tool she'd just seemed to have lost interest in as she added, "I wish they hadn't told you not to hunt for Zenobia anymore. I don't mean because it gave us this chance to be silly. I can't remember the last time it felt this good. But you said something about hoping to capture those other sillies without hurting anybody, and some of those old bearded men out by that farm looked sort of mean.''

He assured her, ''Lots of Mormons grow beards with no malice intended. As a matter of fact, your sister and those boys are less likely to wind up lynched, tarred and feathered, or beat up really bad once they give up to those sober Mormons and disciplined troopers than they might in a few other parts of the West. They tell a sad tale about a sixteen-year-old boy named Charlie McIntyre who got strung up by vigilantes out by Belmont, Nevada, just for *watching* a gunfight.''

Longarm wrinkled his nose and continued. ''What makes it worse is that nobody was killed in the gunfight. Poor young Charlie was just standing there when another kid he knew winged an older mining man called Sutherland. The two boys ran off. So the sheriff tracked them to an abandoned mine and brought 'em back to town. That's when the vigilantes who called themselves the 301 Movement busted into the jail to string both boys from the rafters. So all in all, I'd say your big sister and her playmates would be better off in the hands of those Mormon lawmen or military police.''

She said, ''I hope you're right. How long do you expect it to take? How long can I expect you to be here in Salt Lake City while I wait?''

Longarm wistfully replied, ''Not long, in answer to both questions. Those kids are being led along the primrose path by somebody slick. I suspect one of those three cavalry troopers has some training in the habits of Mister Lo. But they're pushing their luck, breaking cover as those two bodies they left us have barely gone stiff. It was reckless or mighty desperate to stop that coach this afternoon while they still have to have some of that two thousand dollars you and the U.S. Army have provided so recently.''

She said, ''They must be desperate. Zenobia has never

been one for saving, and she's probably spent it all by now.''

"On what?" Longarm asked. "There's only six of them left, and that many can eat, drink, and so on for, say, ten or twelve dollars a day.''

She said, "They must have spent it on something more expensive if they went through two thousand dollars in less than two weeks!''

He muttered, "That's what I just said. I mean to take that gunslick who calls himself Mike Smith back to Denver with me. I can prove he set out to gun a federal officer. Namely me. Sooner or later we'll find out who sent him after me. I'm going to be sort of surprised either way if it wasn't somebody riding with your sister. But it won't really matter, once he appears before my pal, Judge Dickerson of the Denver District Court. Judge Dickerson has been known to order a man insisting his name was John Doe hung by the neck until dead, dead, dead. The judge holds you can't let a crook off just because you can't spell the name on his death sentence right. Allowing that would allow too many crooks an easy out. They hardly ever give their right names to their own pals.''

She asked what he meant about being surprised either way.

He said, "Three different gunslicks tried to keep me from getting out here so the provost marshal who sent for me could tell me my services weren't required. I didn't know who I'd be after before I got here, and Billy Vail never sent me after anybody *else* in the Utah Territory. So when you look at it that way, your big sister or at least one of her pals known to be capable of cold-blooded murder could have been in the market for hired guns.''

She kissed his bare shoulder and asked, "What if you look at it some other way, dear?''

He said, "I already have. How could a wild gal and six wild boys have been expecting me in particular? Major Sullivan was surprised when I showed up, and he remembered

136

my face from an earlier fuss I'd had with his military police. How would outlaws he hadn't told me about have known I'd be the one assigned to their case, even if they'd heard dumb things about my rep as a tracker and took them seriously? When you murder a classmate, burn down your schoolhouse, and rob a safe before stealing seven cavalry mounts, you don't need to wonder whether they're fixing to send some good trackers out after you. If those hired guns had killed me in Rawlins or Ogden, those Mormon and army riders would still be out after them with Indian trackers who grew up tracking *food* in these parts. What could they have worried about me knowing that your average Ho-speaking Digger Indian couldn't figure out?''

Before she could answer, there came another knock on the door. He put a finger to her lips to hush her, and rolled out of bed to wrap a towel around his middle and go to the door. When he saw it was that same Lieutenant Hershey, he stepped out in the hall to keep the officer from spotting the gal in his bed. She sure looked bawdy with the late afternoon sun glowing golden on her unbound hair and naked tits.

So he kept their little secret from the War Department, and cussed a lot when he ducked back in, slamming the door behind him, and announced, ''They got away. Posse riders made it all the way to Kearns and back without seeing them on the road or reading any sign where they could have turned off.''

Minerva smiled in relief and said, ''I told you Zenobia was sneaky! How do you think they managed to vanish into thin air like that?''

Longarm growled, ''I don't know. Neither does Major Sullivan or that local federal marshal. So guess who they just invited back into the club!''

She protested, ''That's not fair. I wanted at least one whole night with you, and didn't you just tell me those Digger Indians could track as good as you could, dear?''

137

He moved to the washstand, tossing aside the towel, and tidied up as he replied with a sigh, "I know what I said. They seem to think I'm better. So they want me to try, and I'm still under orders, damn it."

Chapter 18

Longarm had thought he was tuckered out when he'd gone to bed with Minerva. He was reeling in the saddle by the time they got to Kearns well after dark.

The combined Mormon and military hunting party had set up advance headquarters in the stage company's relay station, which was bigger than anything else in the modest Mormon settlement. Being so close to its Salt Lake City terminal, it wasn't set up to feed and shelter the paying passengers. But having a fair-sized staff to handle its remuda of draft mules, fresh or spent, it had a fair-sized bunkhouse, kitchen, and dining hall to go with the six-hole shithouses, male and female, and it was warm and dry enough for most of the possemen to spread their bedrolls on the surrounding sod, so what the hell.

Longarm unsaddled his borrowed police mount and ran it into the stage line's corral with all the other stock before he and his Winchester got inside to ask what was going on.

Major Sullivan and that Mormon marshal were having buttermilk at the main trestle table in the narrow lamplit dining hall. As Longarm sat down beside the marshal and across from the major, having found a sawhorse for his saddle in the adjoining tackroom, Sullivan said, "Don't ask *me* which way they went. We're hoping you can tell us. You

139

have the rep and . . . well, that delicate matter I'm still not at liberty to talk about seems to have resolved itself and left me free to confide in you more openly.''

An Indian gal dressed like a Mormon housewife set a mug of buttermilk and a slab of marble cake in front of Longarm. So he had to thank her before he asked the military man, ''Which one of your officers stole the slush funds from that safe, Major?''

Sullivan and the Mormon marshal exchanged startled looks. Sullivan sighed and said, ''I told you he was good.''

Then he asked Longarm, ''Who told you?''

Longarm washed down some cake with buttermilk, wishing it could be coffee, and calmly replied, ''A little birdy. That interior guard they winged whilst stealing horses said they were coming from the direction of that burning schoolhouse. Your headquarters building was in the other direction. That one trooper Weems who *could* have known the combination to a safe he wasn't supposed to poke about in *could* have made a wide detour to pick them up some traveling money. But if he *had,* Zenobia Lowell wouldn't have had to wire home for a measly two hundred dollars, and even if she had, they'd have had to be mighty dumb or just plain desperate to stop that stagecoach earlier today. If they were all that dumb, they should have been caught by now! So that leaves desperate, and how desperate would you be with two thousand dollars all told after less than two weeks on the owlhoot trail?''

He swallowed more cake and continued. ''That wicked schoolmarm and her depraved students never spent any of their funds, great or small, on hired guns. To begin with, they've proven perfectly capable of doing their own killing, and after that, none of them had any way of knowing I'd be on my way out here to give you boys a hand. So I reckon I owe one of your delicate army officers for those close calls in Rawlins and Ogden. Who was the son of a bitch? Major Robbins?''

Sullivan shot Longarm a warning look. Longarm put a

140

friendly arm around the shoulders of the older federal man seated beside him on the plank bench and said, "Aw, the marshal here gets to read any and all field notes filed by any of us deputies, and it was your Major Robbins who tried to sell me the notion Trooper Weems had had access to that big safe they'd left *him*, not Weems, in charge of. I can see why you and your general didn't want to let on you suspected anything before you had some proof. But what did you expect us civilian lawmen to do, write a letter to the editor of the *Infantry Journal*?"

Sullivan blanched at the picture and said, "Never mind all that. Never wire half that much money back East to the lady blackmailing you if you don't want your friendly local provost marshal to expose your crude embezzlement either. The officer who made so many mistakes in a row, whoever he might have been, has been allowed to just resign his commission rather than face a court-martial and dishonorable discharge. His name escapes me. Can't we let it go at that?"

Longarm polished off the last of the cake and washed it down with the last of his buttermilk before he replied. "You all might be willing to let it go at that. I can see he had nothing to do with burning down buildings, murdering three people, or stealing seven horses. But there's still the little matter of his sending paid assassins after a federal law officer. Twice."

Sullivan made a wry face and said, "Once he was off the post he was just another civilian, and we don't care what happens to him. If you think you can prove a thing, you're welcome to try. That's not my job, but what if I told you I've been monitoring all the telegraph messages and even steaming open private letters since the night of the murder, arson, and robbery?"

Longarm said, "I'd need a court order to get away with that. There are times I wish I could go by martial law in a partly occupied federal territory. What do you want for a peek at that rascal's private messages, Major?"

Sullivan said, "Your help in tracking down those other scamps. As I assume young Hershey told you when I sent for you again, we've lost them as if they'd ridden off into the sky on six steel-shod cavalry mounts! Few indidual hoof marks of any sort can be picked out on the coach road, which has been pounded since the last rare rain by heavy traffic. But they had to stay on the road unless they turned off it. Only somehow, they didn't. Before you ask why they couldn't have just backtracked this far and ridden on through town, they never did. We've canvassed the town and the farmers, red and white, for over a mile all around. How would you have done that, Deputy Long? We heard about you cutting the trail of those Shoshone across slickrock that time."

Longarm smiled modestly and confessed, "You don't follow tracks across slickrock, Major. You ride around it and pick up the trail on the far side. What rides onto slickrock must ride off of slickerock. What did Major Robbins write or wire that makes you think I'd care?"

Sullivan said, "Nothing. Nothing about *you,* to anybody, I mean. He begged and pleaded for this one young lady of color not to go to his wife or his in-laws with some indiscreet letters he'd written her in the heat of a jealous passion. Putting it bluntly, I don't think the poor simp thinks far enough ahead to have worried about you, and if he'd been in the habit of hiring assassins, why on earth would he have been paying blackmail from the post operating funds?"

Longarm yawned and said, "I'll ask him. The jails of this great land would be empty if nobody ever did anything stupid. But first things coming first, I'll see what I can come up with about those *other* dumb folks after a good night's sleep. I sure ain't up to scouting for sign in the moonlight that your Paiute trackers couldn't read in daylight, even if I was wide awake."

Nobody argued. He got up, went back to the tackroom, and got his bedroll. Then he and his Winchester bedded down upwind of the corral and some smoky night fires burning closer to the station.

It seemed no time at all before some son of a bitch was clanging a breakfast triangle, infernal redwings were twisting door chimes all around, and the sun was not only up, but threatening to really fry them all crisp before noon. So he got up, and discovered to his mild surprise that the spring was back in his legs again.

Not having any morning coffee when a man was used to morning coffee left him cussing the Salt Lake Temple as he nursed a dull headache.

He was dying for a smoke too, and he *had* some cheroots on him. But he didn't want to offend any of the Saints all around as he stuffed his gut with buckwheat cakes, sausages, and more of that gawddamned buttermilk. So he was scowling hard at nothing much when that Indian gal who'd just served him breakfast, after offering him cake the night before, caught up with him out on the shady side of the station as he was washing up at a yard pump. He had shaving soap and a razor in his saddlebags, but he felt sure he'd get by for the day with his stubble clean.

The soberly dressed Indian gal had a wilder-dressed and prettier Indian gal, or breed, in tow. The second one wasn't really dressed in the costume of her nation. She wore a fringed deerskin dress gathered at the waist by a coin-silver concha belt. Paiute, male or female, tended to go bare-ass naked.

All the nations of the Great Basin seemed to speak the same Uto-Aztec dialect they themselves called *Ho*. But their ways of living varied some. To the north roamed the warlike Bannock and Shoshone, mounted, befeathered, and painted much like their Absaroka and Lakota enemies. To the east roamed the mountain deer hunters dubbed Ute or Highlanders by *their* enemies of the Navaho persuasion. They talked, and thought of themselves as, Ho too. The Hopi, or Peacable Ho, lived another way entirely to the south. Then there were the Paiute, or Digger Indians, to the west, roam-

143

ing the vast basin-and-range dry lands on foot with little more than digging wands as their bare asses hung out.

Digger Indians didn't deserve the contempt they were held in by many whites and other Indians. It took brains to eke a living out of a land no others, red or white, could cross without supplies and water from other parts to see them through. The Paiute didn't wander on foot because they didn't know any better. They rode horses where horses could be kept alive on such stark range. They got by with little in the way of baggage or even duds because a man, woman, or child had to travel light when water holes could be eighty miles apart and they had to walk every step of the way under a desert sun. So he'd have taken the two gals who'd just joined him by the pump for a more prosperous breed if they hadn't both worn their black hair in parted Paiute bobs with the same yucca-fiber headbands. The one dressed more Indian had on a pair of yucca-cord sandals as well.

The gal who worked there got right to the point. She said, "Hear me. This is my mother's brother's daughter. She is called Puhahotey. I just told her I thought you were the one our people call Saltu ka Saltu. I heard the blue sleeves calling you Longarm. Is that who you are? Do you know what I am talking about?"

Longarm knew what she was talking about. He wiped his face dry with his kerchief, and ticked his hat brim to the younger one, who had more than a little white blood in her. He said, "Some of your kith and kin have honored me with that term, Miss Medicine Singer. I'm at your service if you'd like to tell me what this is all about."

The little brown gal with sort of elfin Irish features gravely told him, "I think I see why they call you the stranger who is not really a stranger. When I was little, some blue sleeves rode through our camp and shot men, women, and children who had done nothing, nothing. We get along better with the bearded ones who never smoke. But even *they* say bad things about us when we are only trying to help. Our world can be cruel, away from shade and water. Sometimes even those who know it can get in trouble out between the water holes. But when any of you *saltu* get in trouble, the rest of you go crazy, crazy, and we have to be very careful about who we talk to.''

Longarm kept his tone deliberate as he stared off at some buzzards hovering in the distance and quietly asked if she had any secrets to confide in a *saltu* who hardly ever went out of his mind that early in the day and cold sober.

She looked around uneasily and said, ''They tell a story about you scouting for the blue sleeves to the north when the Bannock rose under Buffalo Horn and tried to kill the iron horses running across their hunting grounds. They say the other *saltu* were very angry and acting crazy because some of them had been hurt by the Bannock. They say some of them said the only good Indian was a dead Indian, and that they were about to ride over some Paiute when you got between the two parties and drew your gun. They say you told a blue sleeve with eagles on his shoulders that he had fucked his own mother and that you would kill him if he rode down harmless Digger Indians. We are not harmless and we don't like to be called Diggers. But the Ho who were there thought you had a good heart, for a fucking *saltu*.''

Longarm smiled thinly and replied, ''That's very kind of you, Miss Medicine Singer. But you never rode in to talk to me about long ago and far away, did you?''

She said, ''No. We have more trouble at the homestead claim left to us by my *saltu* father. You people inherit from your father's side. So when he died, I told my mother to ride into the city and talk to them about it at the land office. They told her I was right. I can read, and sometimes this can be a very good *puha*!''

He nodded and said, ''I've noticed the same thing, Miss Medicine Singer. The law is the law, when you can follow its drift, and if you know who I am you know I follow the spirit as well as the letter of the law when it comes to anyone in a fix, red or white.''

She hesitated, then said, ''It is a white woman I have come to you to talk about. She is the one in this fix you speak of. We have given her mustard blooom and willow bark. It doesn't seem to be helping and we are afraid she will die on us, and then what will we tell you *saltu*? How are we going to keep you from thinking it was our idea to shoot her and let her die, without one of your *saltu* medicine men, just because we had to obey the wishes of a guest?''

Longarm said, ''I don't think you and your kinfolk did anything wrong, Miss Medicine Singer. It sounds to me as if that shotgun messenger who said he'd winged one of the road agents who'd stopped him yesterday was on the money. You say it was the *gal* riding with the gang he got?''

The Indian gal nodded gravely and replied, ''In the small of her back. Four balls of double-O buck. She was all right when they rode in at sundown yesterday. We offered them shelter for the night because we knew the younger boys, Willy and Sammy. They had both prospected for yellow iron down this way when school was out over at Fort Douglas. They had always seemed friendly. Last night, they didn't tell us they were hiding from the law. They said they were on their way to some friend's mine off to the west. We let them stay overnight, and only one of them, an older blue sleeve, said bad things about the way we smelled to him. I could see the woman with them was not well. I gave her medicine. It didn't help. I didn't know she'd been wounded until the men she'd been riding with rode on and left her on our hands. Hear me, she is going to die in my bed, if she has not died already, and you have to tell us what to do!''

Longarm nodded soberly and said, ''*Hou ai*. How far away is this place where you've been hiding this wounded outlaw gal?''

She said, ''A little over an hour's ride, out on the flats where the ones who never smoke don't care to plant corn.

But hear me, I don't want these others to know. If I say I will take you to her, you must say you will come alone."

Longarm quietly replied, "I thought that was already understood, Miss Medicine Singer."

Chapter 19

Longarm told the cousin, who was staying where she worked, not to know if anybody else asked about where he might be that morning. Medicine Singer had ridden in on a runty buckskin, and rode it bareback and astride when she and Longarm drifted up the road a piece and lit out through a quarter mile of irrigated pasture and then more sage and cheat grass.

The homestead proven and left to his lawful Indian kin by a white dreamer with a common name and no other visible means of support lay an impractical distance from any road for a truck or dairy farm. As they rode in on the long low ramshackle layout of logs, adobe, and rusty corrugated iron, Longarm spied seven larger chestnuts among the thirty or more head of scrub ponies milling in the big log-railed paddock, excited by the two critters loping toward them in the dusty sunlight.

The impractical herd of riding stock for either a farm or cattle spread were not the only critters excited by their hoofbeats. A sort of impractical number of Paiute, with all sorts of clothes and of every age from bare-ass babes to old gray mummies wrapped in thin trade blankets, came out in the sunlight to stare silently but tensely while Medicine Singer led Longarm into the dooryard and called out in Ho.

You usually saw yellow dogs, a lot of yellow dogs, around an Indian camp or more regular residence. But dogs barked, or howled back at coyotes or the moon late at night. So Longarm had a clearer picture of the reasons for the family's concerns.

Being Indians, most of them knew how it would look, and how whites of any persuasion might come down on them if it looked as if they'd let a white woman die out this way unreported.

Being dealers in shady livestock, if not outright stock thieves, they'd likely come to some understanding with the nearby powers that might be. But anyone could see those were U.S. Cavalry mounts they had over yonder, and a lawman with a rep for not being picky had a mighty narrow line to walk just now.

Not wanting to lose his rep with Indians who gossipped far and wide about such matters between the Rockies and Sierra Madres, nor wanting to be accused as a horse thief by the U.S. War Department, Longarm chose his words as two little bare-ass boys came out into the yard to take the reins of their lathered ponies when they dismounted.

He told Medicine Singer, "It's a good thing that those wanted thieves traded all seven of those stolen army horses with you for fresh ponies. You and your kith and kin were smart not to resist them because they had already killed three people, two of them women, and held up that stagecoach. I will write a note to the remount officer over at Fort Douglas, and I am sure he will give you a reward for recovering them for him. I think that would be a better move for you than trying to sell them to anybody else. Some longbeard who knew they were army horses might buy them from you cheap and then turn them, and you, in for the bounty. It is up to your elders, of course. I won't say anything if they want to just hold on to stolen stock wearing army brands."

She likely repeated some of those suggestions as she spoke to her kin while she led him inside. It was dark and

149

smoky inside. Indians from most nations seemed less bothered by smoky eyes than anyone else, and it did cut down on flies and skeeters.

The not-quite-square structure—you could hardly call it a house and it was too big for a hovel—had more than one room, although all the floors were packed dirt, covered by rush mats and furnished mostly with baskets of all sizes and floor pallets of both machine- and handwoven blankets. The gal who looked a lot like the one he'd been making love to the evening before, only older and scrawnier, lay atop a pile of wool blankets under a robe of rabbit skins cut in thin furry strips and then loosely woven into a big square. She was naked under it. She was flushed and sweating like a pig. But as Longarm hunkered down beside her and raised the robe for a look at her wounds, she rolled her head and gasped, "Don't do that, Tim! It's freezing in here and I'm already so cold I can't stand it!"

Longarm thought without taking out his notes, and decided she was talking to Trooper Tim Garner, who'd deserted alone with Klein and the Trooper Weems that lying officer had accused of robbing the safe.

Medicine Singer murmured, "That fever came over her during the night. My *umbea* says your thoughts about those army horses are *hou*. If you will say on paper that we have done nothing wrong, nothing, she says you can fuck me, or any girl here you like better."

Longarm gently rolled the injured white girl partly on one side as he quietly replied, "Let's eat this apple a bite at a time. I see what you mean about that buckshot. I ain't sure they could do much for her in a hospital at this late date. At least one ball hulled her guts and let her last meal leak into her body cavity. That's how come the fever came on so suddenly. They call this condition peritonitis. It ain't a good condition to have."

He moved the fevered, delirious gal into a more comfortable position, and covered her with the fur-strip robe some more as she complained to him about how dark and cold it was. It wasn't all that bright in there, but it was still the Utah desert in high summer. He took one of her hands and held it as he murmured, "Just try to rest easy, Miss Zenobia. There ain't much we can do for you if that fever don't break on its own."

He glanced up at the Indians gathered around and confided to Medicine Singer, "It could happen. Lord knows, that ain't likely. But what else can we do for her?"

The younger breed gal said, "Nothing. We have given her all the *puha* drinks we give for the crazy hot sweating. I do not think she is going to get better. Will you tell them on paper that we did not shoot her?"

He said, "They know who shot her. That shotgun messenger was proud he had. Let me see if I can get anything out of her about that robbery."

He couldn't. He tried talking sense to the dying schoolmarm. She said she wanted him to hold her close and help her get warm.

He took her in his arms, robe and all, and when one of the Indian kids snickered, one of the older women shushed him with a warning hiss. Zenobia felt much lighter in his arms than her more well-endowed younger sister, and even if she'd been as shapely as her younger sister, the disgusting life she'd been living up to getting buckshot would have discouraged most decent men from wanting more of her.

But she sobbed, "Kiss me, Tim, and hold me tighter. It's so cold in here and I feel so . . . empty. It's as if I have nothing left of me from those little holes in my back down. Do you think I could have caught some infection? Do you think it's going to interfere with my pleasure?"

To which Longarm could only reply, "We'll see. Where were we headed when you first commenced to feel so poorly, ah, honey?"

She answered in a faint whisper, "You're asking *me*? You were the one who knew about that Hasty Cutter we had to get to before they figured out how we'd slipped through Kearns yesterday. Don't you remember? I thought you and those army brats were ever so smart to trick those old Mormons that way!''

He said, "I thought it was slick of us too. Let's see if I have it straight. Young Callahan and Kraft, being known to the folks in Kearns from earlier rides off the military reserve, each drifted through town with one or two others at a time. You and me rode through as a young couple out on a courting ride. Nobody saw the half-dozen riders they were expecting to spot in a bunch, right?''

She didn't answer. She couldn't answer. He lowered her dead form to the pallet and drew the robe over her face before he got out his notebook and stub pencil, telling Medicine Singer, "I'm going to give your kin some messages for them to give to the other *saltu*. We had a few things wrong about this unfortunate and her playmates. But they already have a good lead on me, and I ain't got time to wait around.''

He got back to his feet, asking whether the five surviving members of the gang had been trailing spare mounts as they rode out earlier.

Medicine Singer said they'd only swapped the seven army mounts for five Indian ponies. He smiled wolfishly and said he'd need two really good trail ponies, adding, "I want you and your kind to understand I'm paying cash. I'm leaving that jaded police pony here for safekeeping. It ain't mine to trade. I could sure use any water bags you can sell me. How much for the stock and bags enough to pack twenty-five gallons of water?''

Medicine Singer burbled at her kin some more. Then she said, "We do not ask more than that you bring the ponies and water bags back when you no longer need them. But hear me, Saltu ka Saltu, that is a lot of water. It will weigh more than I do!''

He headed outside as he told her, "That can't be helped. Water runs eight pounds a gallon, and it can take a heap of gallons for a man and his critters from one water hole to another further west. My best bet for heading them off is that they don't seem to know as much about the country as the rest of us. The way things are shaping up, that wicked schoolmarm inside was only the mighty common interest the gang formed around. It looks as if Trooper Tim Garner was calling most of the shots. We'll know more about who shot whom once we round the young rascals up.''

Squinting against the sun dazzle outside, Longarm turned to the west to stare hard at the horizon and mutter, "Not a sign of dust. Not that you'd expect any at this late date. Those two army brats, free to ride off on overnight expeditions without having to ask their first sergeant for a pass, would have been reliable guides this far southwest of the fort. But still living at home, they wouldn't know any routes across these sage flats to the Cedar Mountains that the rest of us can't figure out with our common sense and eyeballs. So west of here, it's safe to figure Tim Garner is leading the way as well as calling the tune when it comes to blood and slaughter.''

Medicine Singer followed him to the paddock rails, pointing with her chin and saying, "Let me pick out four ponies. They have been broken in our way. I don't have to chase them all over with a throw rope the way you cruel *saltu* like to.''

Longarm said, "They're your ponies. But what's all this about you rounding up more than two? One for me and my saddle, with another to lead under the lighter load of water and swap to now and again.''

She said, "I am riding with you. You said you wanted to beat those bad boys to the Cedar Mountains. It is true they are only a hard day's ride west across what looks like flat open range. But hear me, it is not so flat everywhere. There are deep dry washes. There are salt flats. One really big one you don't want to try and cross between here and those mountains. If you know where you are going, you will get there sooner. If you don't know where you are going, you could end up having to backtrack, if you were lucky. There is quicksand under the biggest salt flat. I can lead you

153

straighter than you would ever find your way alone. I have been to the Cedar Mountains and beyond, on horseback and on foot. Sometimes it gets too hot for horses over that way. But that is the best time to hunt antelope and rabbit.''

By then most of the other Indians had followed them outside. So as soon as Longarm grudgingly agreed, Medicine Singer recruited two of her small bare-ass brothers, cousins, or whatever to help her round up the riding stock the two of them would need.

As they did so, Longarm got out his notebook and tore out a couple of pages to write a message to that marshal from the Salt Lake District Court. Longarm knew Major Sullivan would get to read it. But the marshal was his nominal superior in these parts, and it would serve the military police right if they had to ask other federal riders what was going on.

With all those willing extra hands, the Indian in-laws of Medicine Singer's late and shady white father made short work of getting two ponies haltered and laden with water bags. They put his saddle and bridle on a spunky little black-maned buckskin. Medicine Singer's paint wore an Indian bridle, but she preferred to ride bareback, and Longarm had to allow that would be easier on her paint as the day wore on and the sun rose higher.

While some of them had been helping with the horseflesh, others had carried the dead gal outside, wrapped in that same rabbit-fur robe, and set her down in the middle of the door-yard, ready to be picked up by anyone who might want her. Had they not been living half white, or half trash white at any rate, they'd have left her inside and moved away. But it got tougher to follow old-time traditions as you cluttered your life up with notions that cost real money and had bills of sale and deeds attached to them.

Longarm allowed that the late Zenobia Lowell would keep almost as well in the sun for as long as it took them to get word about her into Kearns. But as they made sure their water bags were secure, he casually asked the breed gal if her more distant kin over at the Skull Valley Agency still followed the ways of most Ho speakers when it came to dead bodies.

She shook her head and said, "They can't. That reservation is too small for anyone to move really far when there is a death in the band. They have to let the agents who feed them bury their dead in the earth as if they were *saltu*. Those of us who would rather live free and feed ourselves have to act even more like *saltu*, as you know. If we all went away and left this proven homestead to my dead father and that dead woman across the yard, we would have to start all over, and it takes you five years to prove a homestead, even when you are pure *saltu* and the people at the land office do not argue with you."

He said, "I just said they'd have her body off your property before sundown if your kin get this message to town sometime today."

He handed her the pages from his notebook and added, "Let's you and me get going the other way, if you really mean to tag along."

She passed the paper on to an older boy, but said, "Hear me. It is going to be very hot and dry before noon and there is something I do not understand."

Longarm got a good grip on both his mount's reins and the lead line of the blue roan packing his water as he asked what she was mixed up about.

She said, "You keep saying we have to beat those others across the desert to the Cedar Mountains. But they did not tell us where they were going. They did not tell *you* where they were going. So what makes you think you know where they are going?"

Longarm pointed with his jaw at the fur-covered form on the bare dirt across the dooryard as he told Medicine Singer, "*She* did. You were there. Let's ride."

They mounted up and rode as all her Paiute kin yelled and waved at them. Medicine Singer waited until they were out of earshot before she called out, "I know I was there. I heard nothing, nothing about the way they were riding. She only said that if your name was Tim you were riding to meet somebody named Hasty Cutter."

Longarm nodded and replied, "We had her down as the ringleader when in point of fact she only had one thing on her mind most of the time. Hasty Cutter makes little sense as the name of a partner in crime. But they call the dumb way west, around the south shores of the Great Salt Lake, Hastings Cutoff, and Lord knows those boys have been riding dumb for close to two weeks now."

Chapter 20

Lansford Hastings was the name of the greenhorn who'd published a guidebook to the Far West without knowing all that much about it. It was easy to see on any map that the wagon routes over the South Pass to Fort Bridger swung way the hell north to Fort Hall on the Snake River plains, then split up to form the Oregon and California Trails, depending on where a wagon train wanted to end up. So Hastings hadn't been the first to suggest cutting off some time and distance by leaving the sure water along first the Bear, then the Snake or Humboldt Rivers. Some parties saved days on the trail, in wetter years, taking the Soda Springs Cutoff well short of Fort Hall, if they were headed for California, and beelining across the sage flats north of the Great Salt Lake to the headwaters of the Humboldt, over two hundred miles to the west. A few wagon trains, as well as the later and more direct stage and railroad routes, ran from Fort Bridger down into the Mormon Delta to reprovision, and then pushed around to the north of the lake where the going was easier. Or at least not as bad.

But Hastings had seen a better way with his pencil, and laid out his notorious four-hundred-miles-shorter route around the south shores of the lake and across country never intended for man or beast to walk across.

As Longarm and Medicine Singer rode well south of the line drawn on Lansford Hastings's fool map, the pretty Paiute breed explained how long fingers of treacherous salt pans, dried-out bays of a once bigger lake, thrust south of the present shorelines for as much as twenty miles just north of Skull Valley. All those skulls you saw along the uncertain stream running north to the lake from the springs at the Indian agency were the remains of critters who'd made it that far in the dry months, only to find the streambed bone-dry.

After you detoured around or made it across more than one salt flat, you had to get over or squeeze past the north end of the Cedar Mountains, where the long jagged-ass fault-block petered out along the west shore of the lake, so you could push on across the Great Salt Desert. It was ten days by ox-team or a two-day ride on horseback over almost pure table salt without a break, unless you broke through where groundwater came bubbling up through quicksand.

Medicine Singer said once you got to the other side of the Great Salt Desert, it was only thirty miles to the nearest water, across bare rocky ridges and more sagebrush and cheat.

He said he hoped to head the gang off where the Hastings Cutoff had to bottleneck between the Cedars and the lake. He asked if she thought greenhorns who didn't know the Cedars could ride directly over them.

She answered, "I don't know. None of us have ever tried. There is nothing on the other side but the Great Salt Desert. Crossing it where there are wagon ruts, telegraph poles, and those Central Pacific tracks can be bad enough. There is nothing to hunt, and a lot of places to get in trouble, out on all that wide flat emptiness. I think they will skirt the aprons of the Cedar Mountains too. If they know what is good for them, they will ride north along the lake until they come to the iron horse's tracks across the north end of the salt flats before they turn west again."

Longarm shook his head and said, "Hastings Cutoff

doesn't swing that far north. If it did, I'd still want to avoid those tracks if I was on dodge from three murders and a stagecoach robbery. I'm hoping you're right about the weather in the near future. If they scout for shade and hole up during the worst heat of the day, we ought to make it over to the Cedars ahead of them. Can you beeline us to just miss the south end of that Skull Valley salt flat and get us to high ground by sundown?''

She said, ''No. The mountains are too far and we will kill all four of these ponies if we ride them that fast in this heat. But *they* will kill those *other* ponies if they ride them half as hard. They have no fresher mounts with them to change to. They are not carrying as much water. There are many washes between here and the Cedar Mountains. But when you come to them, you have to stop and dig for the water. I think if I was this wicked Tim, I would want to stop any time now. There are places where desert willow shades sandy washes and clean water lies close to the surface.''

He asked if she was thinking of any such place in particular. Once she told him there were dozens, he allowed it was time to change ponies, water the six of them, and get a move on.

So they did, and she was right about how hot and dry it could get. All four ponies were jaded and listless, with no more water in the bags to give them, when they came at last, after dark, to the lower slopes of the rugged ridge called the Cedar Mountains. It looked as if the big untidy wrinkle ran north and south for forty-odd miles.

But the moon was high and better than half full. And the Paiute breed had hunted in this big old rock pile before, mostly for pinyon nuts, she said. She didn't have to tell Longarm the Indians had less use for the scrub cedar that grew mixed in with the stocky pinyon pine. Paiute who'd overlooked the rape of a daughter or more had been known to kill a white man who'd cut down a pinyon pine for firewood. Having eaten the small sweet white nuts from their cones, Longarm was inclined to side with the Paiute about such things.

Knowing better where they were, Medicine Singer found them a spring at the base of a cliff, with willow and cotton-wood crowded about.

Stock wouldn't browse on willow, but they thought cot-tonwood leaves were salad greens. So a grand time was had by all but Longarm as he worked his way around to the top of the sixty-foot cliff. Once he had, he spotted that one pin-point of firelight right away. When Medicine Singer joined him, saying she'd tethered the stock but hardly expected them to stray from browse and water, he asked her if she knew of any homestead, red or white, out yonder on the flats.

She said, "No. Nobody lives there. There would be no reason to. I think I know the place. There *is* an old wagon trace over that way. I never knew who might have left it. You were right about that being the dumb way to circle the big bitter water to the north. That night fire burns where the bad trail crosses a wooded wash. Willow and cottonwood, the same as below. If those wicked young *saltu* got to it late in the day, when it was really hot and they were having trouble with their own mounts, I can see why they'd stop there for a trail break. But why are they still there? Hear me, that fire is bigger than it needs to be. They are stoking it with fresh wood every few minutes. If they wanted to busy themselves with something smarter, they would have ridden on by this time. Everybody knows you should ride across the desert by night, when everything is cooler. I kept trying to tell you that all afternoon. Now I see why you insisted we ride on like ants atop a hot stove. You knew your *saltu* friends were crazy!"

Longarm said, "They ain't exactly my friends. At least one of them is crazy-mean, and the others have been mean enough to go along with him. They'll likely break camp around dawn, not being smart as you. Can we get on up to where the old Hastings Cutoff swings within rifle range of some higher ground, Miss Puhahote?''

She said, "Call me Medicine Singer in *saltu*. You say our words so funny it makes me want to laugh at you, and I do not think you are a fool. We can beat them to such a good place for an ambush with time to spare. They are not moving and the night is not half over.''

So they went back down to the spring. It was her suggestion they take full advantage of the spring in the time they had to spare. Longarm laughed, started to argue, and decided her notion made a lot of sense.

So they both shucked their duds and jumped into the cool springwater to splash and laugh away the sweat and trail dust they'd picked up riding during the afternoon heat. Medicine Singer dove under, flashing her bare brown ass at the moon. When she came up closer to Longarm with bare tits glittering in the moonlight, something under the water told him it was time they got dressed and moved it on up the road.

Medicine Singer seemed a mite pensive, or at least not as talkative, while they got dressed not looking at one another. They mounted up to follow a contour line north to where a barn-sized boulder had come down a wash, beaching itself high on the alluvial fan and gathering smaller ones around it like a mother hen with her chicks.

Longarm led the way to the natural ambush site. A clump of popple had sprouted upslope of the rock pile to make use of the wetter sand found around the bases of such dew-collecting rock piles. So he and Medicine Singer tethered the ponies where they'd be free to browse, out of sight from the flats below. Then Longarm took his bedroll, a pair of field glasses, and some canned tomato preserves from his saddle, along with his Winchester '73, and scrambled to the flat top of the big mother hen.

Medicine Singer followed and sat on her knees, bemused, as she watched him unroll the bedding across the rock and shift some loose slabs of the layered sandstone to form a low shield for anyone prone on the bedding with or without a rifle.

Off to the east-northeast the Great Salt Lake shimmered in the moonlight to the blurred horizon as its modest waves lapped at a ghostly shoreline of salt-encrusted cobbles and pebbles. To the east-southeast a pie wedge of sage flat thrust north between the lake and the slopes of the Cedars, narrowing to a long rifle shot between Longarm's rifle and the lakeshore, with the trail much closer, hugging the aprons of the range to avoid the marshy shifting shoreline.

Way out where the moon on sagebrush seemed just a dark gray carpet fading away to black in the distance, that pinpoint of campfire still gleamed like a big lonesome star that had fallen on the rug. Even further out, a patch of lighter blackness had to be the salt flats made more dangerous by the runoff from Skull Valley, far to the south.

Longarm set the field glasses and Winchester handy to the loophole he'd left himself in the rock slabs piled near the head of the bedroll. He said to the Indian gal, "That ought to do her for now. Lord willing and they're dumb enough to ride by daylight, I reckon I'll start by dropping their ponies out from under them. I'll be counting on you to recognize riding stock from your own spread. I've never laid eyes on one of the gang, as a matter of fact, and this would be a bad time and place to smoke up innocent riders!"

She asked in an injured tone, "Do you think I am ugly? Or is it because my mother was a Ho?"

Longarm had to chuckle at the possible double meaning of her dumb question before he asked her what had made her ask such a dumb thing.

She said, "I could see you were hard when we got out of the water back there. You heard that my *umbea* said it was all right to fuck me. Why didn't you want to fuck me when I could tell you felt like fucking *somebody*?"

Longarm was aware of that old familiar feeling in his pants as he soberly assured her, "It ain't that the thought

162

never crossed my mind. If we live through the next few hours I might just take you up on such a generous offer. I slept alone last night, and I can see by your pout that you must have too. But there's a time and place for everything, and I'd sure look dumb in the prone position of an infantry rifleman on top of a pretty gal, no offense.''

She sighed and asked in a tone of childish logic, ''Who could say you looked dumb if nobody else was looking? How do you know we shall *live* through the next few hours? What if they kill us and I never get to say I fucked Saltu ka Saltu?''

He laughed and said, ''Such is the price of fame. Are you saying you were just out to count coup on my old organ-grinder? Has some other Ho gal been saying mean things about my personal habits?''

She answered innocently, ''I heard nothing, nothing about you being mean to Ho women, as some other *saltu* can be. I don't see why any man would promise a woman the moon if she'd fuck him and then beat her all black and blue after she did it!''

He said, ''Neither do I. I reckon their mothers and Queen Victoria have some gents mixed up about natural feelings.''

Medicine Singer sat up to unfasten her concha belt and peel her deerskins off over her head. Then she spoke in a tone that was a bit too conversational for a gal wearing nothing but moonbeams. ''I have read about this Queen Victoria. Why do you people obey her when she gives such crazy orders? I understand why some things must not be done because they are dangerous medicine. But what is wrong with fucking a friend when she is not even a distant relative, has no blood running out of her, and no other man has even offered ponies for her?''

Longarm had to allow he had no sensible excuses by her standards, and he was mighty curious as to whether she did it *saltu* style or like a Ho. So once he'd established she kissed more French than any other style, it only took a few more minutes before they were *both* wearing no more than moonlight and going at it like old pals atop the bedding over a firmer than usual foundation.

As he entered her with her chunky brown rump braced against solid rock, she confided without a trace of shyness that she'd never had such a big *kutsu* probe her that deeply. He told her, truthfully, that he found her an unusual experience as well. It always felt like you were telling the truth when you told the gal you were with at the moment that she was the best lay you'd ever had. It always felt that good, and that was no doubt the reason men always wanted more, bless every sweet pussy a man could get into in the limited time he had to work with as the sands of his life ran through Fate's fickle fingers.

After they'd come in the old-fashioned way, Medicine Singer wanted to get on top. So he let her, and that felt swell too when she planted a sandal to either side and squatted on his beanpole "Chinee Style," as they'd named it out in the Mother Lode Country. There they paid extra for it, whether the gal was yellow, red, black, or white, as long as she knew how to *do* it!

Medicine Singer did, and that was the position she was in when the first light of dawn allowed Longarm to see the color of her firm brown bouncing breasts. He was fixing to come again when she suddenly froze, with his trembling manhood way up inside her, while she stared off in the distance.

He asked, "What's the matter? Got a cramp? Want me to get on top for a spell?"

She began to move again as she demurely replied, "That campfire no longer burns. The dust of moving ponies rises against the lighter sky to the east. But we still have time to come again if you want to help. Don't stop now. I can keep an eye on all you *saltu* boys at the same time. So I will tell you when you have to stop fucking and get ready for some fighting!"

164

Chapter 21

They had more than enough time, thanks to the deceptive appearance of distances in thin high-altitude air under the big sky of the Great Basin. The sun had risen to gild all those sage flats and rising clouds of pony dust by the time Longarm and Medicine Singer had untangled from one another and gotten dressed again. But those distant riders still rode toward them at some distance, near the wider base of that pie wedge now, as Longarm lay prone with his Stetson in one hand and his field glasses in the other, screening the lenses from the low sun to the east lest a reflected flash give their position away.

Through the glasses he could turn five flyspecks into tiny riders on tiny ponies. They were trotting their mounts in the coolness of the morning, making eight or nine miles an hour as they likely hoped to round the north spur of the Cedars and . . . then what? Head out across a good fifty miles of shadeless white salt in the heat of high noon?

He told Medicine Singer, "I make it three buckskins, a paint, and a roan. No pack ponies. Who might we be talking about, and can you think of anywhere more sensible they could be headed?"

She peeked over the low rock barrier and said, "Those are the five ponies we had to trade for those seven army mounts, whether we wanted to or not. If they ride up the west shore of the big bitter water far enough, they may be able to get fresh water, or board a train where the iron horse stops where Dove Creek dies in another salt flat.''

Longarm swept further out with the field glasses as he muttered, ''I have a heap of questions I'd like to ask those boys, starting with who might be calling the shots. Those horny schoolboys, Callahan and Kraft, saw that wicked schoolmarm first. But it's usually the older boys who wind up leading gangs, and you'd think two kids who've ridden off on overnight trips in this country would know better.''

He adjusted the field glasses to focus further out as he went on, half to himself. ''That dying schoolmarm seemed to favor the army man called Tim Garner, and we know all of them to be sort of impulsive. An old army man who thought he knew it all would be more inclined to tell anyone who tried to tell *him* anything to shut up. It's easy to think you know it all when you don't know much. That's how come we call such greenhorns greenhorns. Could I borrow one of those silver conchas off your belt, honey?''

She allowed she'd take everything off again if he wanted. Longarm kept the field glasses trained on a fainter haze of distant dust as he held out his hand to her, saying, ''It's getting too hot for riding of any sort. Don't you get sweaty in that deerskin on days like this?''

She slipped a concha off the two thongs they were strung on as she said, ''You sweat and the thirsty air sucks it away no matter what you have on out here on the sage and salt flats. Deerskin is only a little warmer by day, and much warmer after dark when the chill breezes blow toward the great bitter water. What are you going to do with this, beloved *hona*?''

He set the field glasses aside, and rose higher on his elbows as he peered through one of the slits in the center of the dished coin silver disc at that further dust cloud, explaining, ''If your kin got my message to the posse leaders, that could be them out yonder following our trail from your

166

spread if I've got my directions sorted right. Or they could be somebody else just out to avoid that big salt pan north of Skull Valley the same as we did. Either way, they're swinging south and I'd like to talk them out of that if I can."

He shot a glance at the much closer riders, made a wry face, and lined the concave side of the concha up first with the low sun behind them and then with the base of that distant dust cloud. He kept rocking the silver disc up and down until the girl who owned it asked what he thought he was doing.

He said, "I hope I'm reflecting a sunbeam back at them from this darker hillside as I wiggle and jiggle. I can't tell just who or where I'm aiming at. But as I sweep across their general direction by hook and by crook, it ought to flash in their eyes, somewhere along my arc, as dots and dashes of dazzle, depending on how fast I pivot up or down."

She said, "I have seen sunlight gleaming from a distant piece of glass or metal. Are you trying to make them look this way? It is too far for them to see anything very well."

He said, "I know. I'm telling them who we are, where we're at, and why in Morse code. The army signals in Morse by heliograph or shuttered sun mirrors out here where the sun shines so much, no offense. So I'm hoping there's at least one soldier blue over yonder who reads Morse. If there ain't, we're no better off than we were. You say there's no other easy way for those five owlhoot riders to get over this range of wooded fault blocks, honey?"

She said, "If there was, nobody would have blazed that trail around to the north end of the Cedars. All that water you see along the other side is bitter water. Too bitter to drink. Too bitter for fish. With swarms of biting salt flies all along the shores. I think they are trying to get to the trail of the iron horse. I don't see how they can hope to cross the really wide salt to the west and go on, and on, to the fresh water at Snake Springs, a day's ride on past the salt flats!"

167

Longarm went on signaling as he muttered, "The Central Pacific has mapped that water stop as Cobre, meaning Snake in Spanish. They likely thought that sounded more reassuring to passengers. I said I meant to ask those boys a heap of questions. So let's not worry about where in blue blazes they think they're going. Let's just see if we can keep 'em from getting there."

He handed back her concha. He didn't need the field glasses to make out the colors of the ponies those five survivors were riding now. They were well toward the narrower end of the pie wedge, but still close to seven furlongs out, when they suddenly reined in and gathered their mounts tight for what seemed a consultation.

Longarm muttered, "I was afraid some of *them* had some basic cavalry training too. They must be worried about somebody up this way with a scoped plains rifle. Lord knows I can barely cover the trail where it passes close with this poor puny Winchester .44-40. I make the range to the trail a tad over four hundred yards downslope. I wish it was way less. I could win you a turkey at two hundred with this seventy-three, but you sure need luck past four hundred, and I'll be in even more trouble if they ride single file along the lake shallows."

Medicine Singer said, "One of them is riding closer alone."

Longarm swore under his breath and replied, "I noticed. I was afraid somebody had been through Cavalry Basic. Ever since Little Big Horn, a patrol leader is supposed to hedge his bets by sending just a single target to scout likely ambush sites, and I could see by moonlight that this rock pile dominated the flats as far as the lakeshore."

He reached for the field glasses again and trained them on that more distant dust. He couldn't tell whether they'd changed direction or even noticed his attempts at heliographing.

He hauled out his six-gun and held it out to his Paiute companion, saying, "We have to see if we can hold them

168

a fair spell. It won't be easy. I'd be much obliged if you'd take this revolver—I'll give you some extra rounds—and see if we can convince them there's a bigger bunch of us.''

She said she didn't think she could hit anything with a pistol at the range of the trail passing below them. He told her what he wanted her to try. She laughed like a mean little kid and took the six-gun as he dug out a handful of extra .44-40 rounds.

After she'd slid down the uphill side of the boulder, and made sure of the four ponies while she was at it, Longarm turned his attention back to that lone rider moving in to scout their position, blast his nosy soul. As Longarm watched along the sights of his Winchester, the rider on one of the buckskins reined in about three furlongs or six hundred and sixty yards out to draw his own saddle gun, a son-of-a-bitching Springfield .45-70 with a much slower rate of fire but twice the range of a Winchester.

As the distant stranger dismounted and loosely tethered his mount to a clump of sage, Longarm muttered, ''I know just how you feel right now. But that don't mean I have to feel sorry for you, you son of a bitch! Two of the folks the bunch of you killed outright were women, and you didn't show much consideration for the others aboard the coach you stopped either!''

The advance scout began to move to his left up the ever-steepening slope with his army rifle held at port arms. He was one of those three deserters, it seemed clear. He knew what he was doing. Worried about a big rock pile ahead, he meant to work his way to higher ground, out of range, and have a peek down at it, as if he was a big-ass bird!

Longarm didn't want that to work. He gathered up the blankets and his other gear to ease his way down the far side. Then he moved the four ponies around to the north face of the bigger boulder. They were now visible to any-body down along the lakeshore trail, but the mountain-climbing son of a bitch with that army rifle wasn't *on* the lakeshore trail. If he didn't spot Medicine Singer farther up the slope, he'd either head back to report the way forward clear, or he'd scout in on foot close enough to be captured and held quiet, out of the others' sight.

Longarm had a clear view to his right up the wash he'd asked his pretty Paiute breed to see if she could work her way up. He couldn't see her up yonder. Kids who grew up Paiute could be hard to see when they didn't want you to see them. Longarm worked his way back around the base of the rock until he could peek at that distant white scout through the gap between the main boulder and the tangle of popple behind it. The cuss was scaling the rocky slope with some skill, keeping his balance as dry scree rolled out from under his boots to cascade on down raising dust. Longarm was hoping he'd either work higher, decide there was nobody over this way and turn back, or move over to the wash and slide down it like a fly coming into the spider's parlor. At close range Longarm's Winchester had it over that long-range single-shot army rifle. Longarm was wishing there was some way to signal Medicine Singer. If she was further up when their advance scout made it to the wash, she'd be in no danger as long as she kept her head down. He'd only asked her to cause some confusion with other gunsmoke. So she was likely confused now, the poor little thing.

The advance scout changed course once he was higher than the top of the rock where Longarm and Medicine Singer had just made love. He'd started moving in on the rock pile. Longarm knew better. But it felt as if the rascal was staring right at him as the man moved ever closer along the side of the slope.

Then all of a sudden Medicine Singer broke cover, higher up, to rise from a clump of rabbit bush like a cobra coming up out of its basket with Longarm's .44-40 gripped in both hands while all hell broke loose!

Longarm fired his Winchester as the other white man swung the muzzle of his own rifle to cover what he might have taken for a wild Indian. Longarm missed at that range, but the distracted rifleman in the open turned to stare his way, and he who hesitated in a gunfight could be in a whole lot of trouble. For Medicine Singer was blazing away at much closer range, and one of her wild rounds smashed into the scout's head to remove his hat and half his brains.

The gal yelled, *"Hau, hau ai kiyiyiyi!"* as her target rolled ass-over-tea-kettle down the dry slope in a cloud of dust and big loops of bloody foam, to fetch up like a discarded rag doll against the sage at the bottom of the rise.

Longarm whistled and waved the gal in, sure enough, other guns commenced to pop further out on the sage flat. The range was impossible, and the two of them were soon back atop the main rock, without all that bedding but with both guns and his field glasses.

As she lay prone beside him, the pretty breed said, "I did it! I did it! My *puha* is strong today! Today I am a woman who can say she fucked Saltu ka Saltu and killed somebody!"

Longarm said, "Good for you. Give me back my six-gun and keep your head down!"

She did as she was told, asking what he wanted her to do next.

He said, "Ain't much we *can* do, damn it. We can't get at them from here. They can't get at us from there. Come sundown they may try to ride past us out of range. They may try to work around behind us in the dark, or they may just turn around and ride. I sure hope I can keep them from doing that. Whether I can or I can't, it looks as if we could be in for a long hot day up here!"

They were. As the sun rose higher, Medicine Singer slipped back down to gather up his scattered bedroll and break off some popple branches.

As the gang doubtless watched from way out of range, the pretty breed spread blankets for them to recline on and improvised a lopsided but shady shelter from that ground tarp over a crude framework of popple tied with soapweed fiber. Longarm told her not to be silly when she wanted to screw some more. It wasn't *that* cool in the shade as the sun rose higher.

If it had been, he still wouldn't have wanted to be literally caught with his pants down. Those last four members of the wanton class had dismounted and fashioned crude sun shades out yonder as well. They might or might not have given a shit about their ponies. There wasn't a whole lot you could do for a pony tethered on short water rations under a cloudless summer sky in the Great Basin.

So a million years went by, and somebody down yonder must have lost hope of going on, or seen the same dust Longarm was watching through his field glasses while Medicine Singer nibbled his ear and talked to him dirty in Ho. For all of a sudden they seemed to be breaking camp.

Longarm growled, "Shit! You boys can't get up from the table now! This game was just getting interesting!"

Medicine Singer turned to study them a spell before she said, "We won. They don't want to play *nanipka* with us anymore. They are running away. They are afraid of us!"

Longarm grumbled, "I just said that. I don't want them to run away. On the other hand, I have a saddle gun effective at four hundred yards and they have four effective at eight, on wide-open range for them to fan out and cross-fire us. So I reckon we'd best stay put and let 'em ride."

She said, "*Hua!* Does that mean we can fuck some more while they get away?"

Longarm laughed and said, "Not just yet. I never said anything about them getting away. They still have a ways to ride with the lakeshore to one side and the rocky apron of these mountains to the other."

She started to ask what difference that might make. Then she cocked her pretty head and said, "Listen! I think I hear something! I *do* hear something! I hear one of those brass bugles your blue sleeves blow when they are chasing after somebody!"

Longarm replied with a thin smile, "I just said that."

172

Chapter 22

Medicine Singer had heard right. So before noon they were headed back across the flats with the combined military-Mormon posse and the five fugitives. The late Trooper Klein rode facedown across his saddle, thanks to Medicine Singer's lucky head-shot. The four others got to ride sitting up with their hands cuffed behind them after the bunch of them had given up without a fight. Trooper Weems and the two surviving army brats, Callahan and Kraft, agreed Trooper Garner had led them astray after all they'd ever wanted to do was fuck their schoolmarm after classes. The three of them offered to testify at his court-martial that Garner and the more adventurous Zenobia Lowell had tied young Petula Dorman up in the schoolhouse cellar after they'd found out she'd been telling tales out of school. They agreed it had been Tim Garner who'd set fire to the place as they were leaving, and that the tale told by that interior guard Zenobia had gunned by the stable had been the simple truth.

None of the dumb desperate runaways had gone anywhere near that safe in the headquarters building. They'd hid out in a series of empty houses the three nosy schoolboys had come across in their wanderings. The little money Zenobia had gotten from home had about run out when young Bobby

Worthington had started writing home to his own kin. The three willing to testify said they hadn't been there when Tim Garner had ridden with Worthington to meet his mother and then killed them both. They said they'd stopped that stage less than twenty-four hours later because they had to. Willy Callahan confessed he'd stumbled over Medicine Singer's homestead and ragged-ass kin just poking around Kearns on horseback months ago. The pretty breed was willing to back him on that, and said he'd been by again, now and then, with Worthington and Kraft, carrying on silly and trying to get laid without any luck.

Callahan said they'd tried to warn Tim Garner that the tales he'd heard about a Hastings Cutoff out of Utah Territory were optimistic as hell. But since they were headed that way to begin with, and since Zenobia was feeling too poorly to ride on with them in any direction, prudent or not, Garner thought it was their best chance to throw off the pursuit they knew they'd stirred up by then.

That was, damn their hides, about all they had to clear up. This left everyone but them and Longarm reasonably content. Medicine Singer felt a tad wistful about the future she faced with Longarm. But she had some swell brags to count coup on in Paiute circles. The Mormon lawmen felt proud about resolving the robbery of that Mormon-owned stage line, and Major Sullivan was so pleased with himself he was in danger of jacking off in public.

He'd been the one who'd decoded Longarm's improvised heliograph message and ordered a risky but more direct advance across that miles-wide salt flat to cut the fugitives off just in time. Moreover, he was bringing Trooper Garner in for a sure public hanging, and better yet, they wouldn't have to hang those army dependents or even Trooper Weems. The personnel officer was doubtless going to be cheered some by the civilian schoolmarm he'd approved not having to stand trial on any charges now. And all that worry about the one victim being a half-baked Mormon hadn't added up to anything anybody had to worry about.

Longarm was still a tad morose because, in the end, the case of the wicked schoolmarm had added up to no more than one female sex fiend and a half-dozen assholes with hard-ons, driven to acts of desperation by a tattletale.

Try as he might—and those three kids who were willing to talk really did seem willing to talk—he couldn't get a thing out of them about three other assholes he'd shot it out with getting there.

Major Sullivan pointed out, and Longarm had to agree, that that officer who'd really robbed that safe and tried to blame Trooper Weems could simply not have known Longarm was coming to Fort Douglas. Nobody but the provost marshal and the general himself had known they'd sent out for extra help before Longarm had already shot his way through those jaspers in Rawlins and Ogden.

So while it hurt like fire, once they'd all made it back to Salt Lake City after sundown, and since nobody wanted more than a signed deposition from Longarm to present with stronger testimony, he wired Billy Vail he was coming back, and wired Ogden to turn the stubborn Mike Smith loose for lack of evidence.

Then he and Medicine Singer spent the few hours he had before his night train left to say some mighty fond farewells in a brushy vacant lot near the depot. Getting a room in a hotel with a Paiute gal in deerskin could get expensive as well as complicated.

He was just as glad to board the night local well screwed. For the pretty little blonde he got to talking to in the coach seats turned out to be a Saint who'd taken him for a man of the same persuasion. But they parted friendly in the Ogden depot without ever getting to compare underwear, and Longarm holed up in a compartment with a pile of magazines and a fresh-bought notebook so he could write up a neat summation of the case so far while it was fresh in his mind.

He sent out for light grub, and there was running water to mix with his own Maryland Rye in the private compartment. He got off in Cheyenne to change trains the next morning. The Burlington varnish he could have ridden down to Denver wasn't ready to leave yet. It waited for another cross-country flyer from the east so it could carry a profitable passenger load south. But knowing his railroad timetables better than most, he was able to wrangle an earlier ride down to Denver aboard a morning freight train, and got there over an hour sooner than if he'd waited for that passenger train.

So he had time for a bowl of chili con carne on Larimer Street, and that allowed time for somebody from the courthouse crowd to see him back in town and mention it over at the Federal Building.

Marshal Billy Vail still had a time catching up on his own stubby legs. He tried more than one likely place before he found Longarm in the shady doorway of a tobacco shop across from an office building on Wynkoop Street, calmly staring at the entrance across the way.

The portly older lawman joined Longarm there, glancing across the way as he soberly said, "Got your wire. You never said anything about tracking anybody here in Denver. Who are we after?"

Longarm took a drag on his cheroot before he replied, "Ain't sure. Both the mining company inherited by that pretty Widow Muldoon and the law firm retained by her are across the way in that same building. I have some copper badges I borrowed off my pal, Sergeant Nolan, covering the back."

Vail noticed his own cigar had gone out, and groped for a light as he asked, "How come? I thought of that angle right off. But it doesn't work. I got word to Nolan as soon as you wired me from Ogden about all those gunslicks messing with you. You and Nolan were the only ones who can swear under oath you saw the young wife of Ferris Muldoon screwing a man who'd threatened his life on that fresh grave. But nobody's gone after Nolan and he's an easier target, walking the streets of Denver like a big-ass bird!"

Longarm said, "I thought of that, and crossed the widow and her no-doubt many admirers off until I'd been at that process of eliminating you preach for a spell. I eliminated Zenobia Lowell as only the pretty temptation who'd attracted herself a remuda of romantic desperados. Once I was sure her simpleminded gang hadn't known or cared exactly who might be after 'em, I was left with the only other capital case I was mixed up in right now. As I just told Nolan, meaning no disrespect, you just put your finger on why they thought it best to nail me first."

The older lawman, who'd broken Longarm in to begin with, didn't need diagrams drawn on blackboards. He lit his cigar, nodded his bullet head, and said, "They figured they could backshoot Nolan at will. They knew that would alert you to the notion someone could be after you, and how come. So they thought it best to make sure *you* were dead before they went after a lawman closer to the courthouse where that pretty Widow Muldoon they admire will stand trial. She'd have a way better chance of getting off without the two of you testifying to her treachery with a lover who might as well have signed a confession as gone for a gun!"

Vail got his cigar going and asked, "So who are we betting on? Her lawyer or another executive of her husband's mining outfit?"

Longarm shrugged and said, "We'll know better in time. Here comes Mike Smith, whoever he might be, and why don't we crawfish back a tad and let him feel free to call on his pal across the way."

As they both eased back from the sunlit street, Vail regarded the stranger coming along Wynkoop on the shady side in a suit that needed pressing, with that Manhattan .36 Conversion peeping out from under his coattails. Vail demanded, "How did you know he'd be coming this way? I thought you'd followed him here!"

Longarm blew smoke out his nostrils and muttered, "That would have been dumb, no offense. I knew he'd be watching out for anybody tailing him, and the man's a professional sneak. So I had my pals in Ogden time his release so's I could board the eastbound night flyer ahead of him and hole up in a compartment. I got off the wrong side in Cheyenne and caught an earlier freight down whilst he no doubt paced the waiting room keeping one eye peeled for this child. I just told you how come I figured to meet him here.''

Vail said, ''No, you haven't. What would you have done if he'd just stayed aboard that night flier east, or caught one west for that matter?''

To which Longarm replied, ''How? He barely had enough on him to get back to Denver, and I just told you why I figured he'd been hired to kill me by somebody here in Denver at that very address across the way. He never tried to get word to anybody from the Ogden jail. Nobody tried to bail him out or even send a cake with a hacksaw in it to him. So I figured he'd figure they still owed him.''

Vail thought and decided, ''He's surely headed for that entrance on *some* serious business. But don't they usually offer half in advance and the rest when through, the way that gal in the song sold her ring-dang-doo?''

The man who called himself Mike Smith vanished into the office building across the way as Longarm said, ''They *tried* to get me, didn't they? No matter what the deal they made might have been, that last of the three came out almost broke, doubtless chagrined, and knowing a client to turn to for what could be defined as a well-earned bonus or hush money. If he hadn't just turned up, we might never have learned who'd hired the three of them. But I was hoping he might, and he did, and as the old song goes, farther along, we'll know more about it!''

Vail asked, ''What do we do when he comes out? Grab him and make him tell us who he just called on upstairs?''

Longarm said, ''Might be neater to wait and see whether he goes to ground or heads back to the depot with his pay-off. You can't hardly visit anybody in such a fancy office building without getting by some likely innocent secretary

178

who'll doubtless recall your visit to his or her superior."

Vail grinned like a kid fixing to steal apples and said, "I'm so glad to hear you've been paying attention to your teacher, and I reckon I'll have to give you at least a B plus on this test, oh, star pupil of mine!"

Then they both stiffened as the sunlit sky above seemed to echo to the staccato whip snaps of small-bore rapid fire, followed by first an ominous silence, and then the banshee wails of some hystericated female.

Longarm broke cover and drew his .44-40 as he headed across the way, and sure enough, the man calling himself Mike Smith tore out toward him, six-gun in hand and face red with rage.

Longarm threw down on the hired gun, shouting, "Drop that gun and grab some sky, Smith!"

But it was like trying to reason with a mad dog, and so Longarm fired as the man he had the drop on tried in vain to aim his own six-gun at him.

The Manhattan went off, aimed too high to worry anybody, as its owner staggered back to end up flat on his back on the sandstone walk with his boot heels hooked on the curb. Longarm moved in, covering him, as a homely-faced gal with a swell figure dashed out to point down at the man called Smith and shout, "Stop him! He just shot my boss, Mr. Beckson of the Muldoon Land and Mining Company!"

Longarm quietly replied, "We just did, ma'am. Is your boss dead or alive at the moment?"

The dying man at their feet groaned up at them, "He'd better be dead, the son of a bitch! He tried to stiff me after he'd double-crossed me and my pard more ways than one! He never said anything about hiring that gun hand who put you on the prod in Rawlins. As I just accused him, he never meant to pay *any* of us for shooting you and some copper badge. He just now laughed in my face and asked right out who I thought I could go to if the lousy fifty dollars he offered wasn't enough!"

The gal said, "I only heard them arguing in the back.

Then this mean thing shot poor Mr. Beckson, over and over again!''

Billy Vail, who'd joined them, stared down as he said, ''We heard, ma'am.'' Then he turned to Longarm and added, ''It all adds up. Thorpe Pulver, who gunned the late Ferris Muldoon, operated out of their branch in Golden. I reckon the owner's frisky young wife had tea for two with *another* younger mining man whenever she came in to Denver for a change of scene. That ought to be easy to prove, and it makes those charges against you and Sergeant Nolan sound mighty silly !''

Police whistles were trilling around the corner as Longarm finished reloading and put his .44-40 away, saying, ''I reckon you're right.'' Then he gently but firmly took the secretary gal by one elbow and told her, ''I'd like a look around upstairs if you'd be good enough, ma'am. You don't have to go all the way back with me, as long as you stick around so's I can take down a full statement.''

She didn't argue. Billy Vail was tempted to, as the two of them turned to the entrance and he heard Longarm say, ''Mayhaps after we get some of it down on paper here, you'd like to have a bite with me over at the Bonhoff Beer Garden so's we can go into things in more depth.''

As Marshal Billy Vail stared after them, he started to call Longarm back and ask him what in thunder he thought a homely young gal could tell them that they didn't already know.

But he never did. He could see the poor little thing had a swell rear end, and Longarm had just said he'd spent that whole night on a train all alone.

Watch for

LONGARM AND THE RIVER PIRATES

236th novel in the exciting LONGARM series
from Jove

Coming in August!

J. R. ROBERTS

THE
GUNSMITH